Lives Less Valuable

Derrick Jensen

To Drew,

Step outside the lines,

Derrick Jens

9/24/10

Occupy Times

Flashpoint Press
An imprint of PM Press

Cover design by Stephanie McMillan
Text design by Michael Link

Edited by Theresa Noll

10 9 8 7 6 5 4 3 2 1

ISBN: 978-1-60486-045-0
LCCN: 2008934202

Jensen, Derrick, 1960–
Lives Less Valuable / by Derrick Jensen.
p. cm.

Fiction

Flashpoint Press
Published by PM Press
Flashpoint Press Box 903 Crescent City, CA 95531
www.flashpointpress.com
PM Press Box 23912 Oakland, CA 94623
http://www.pmpress.org

Printed in the USA on recycled paper.

Also by Derrick Jensen

Lives Less Valuable
Derrick Jensen

Table of Contents

The dream is always the same. It begins with the slightest feeling of unease, as from a misplaced sound or a sudden silence: the too-quick stopping of birdsong or the scolding of squirrels. Then from Malia a moment of hesitation, that inevitable aversion to the warning she knows she must heed, that resistance to acknowledging an unavoidable reality. Each time in the dream she pays attention not to the sound nor to the silence, but to the red-tinted lettuce leaves in her garden, and to her weeding. She pays attention to her niece Robin, and notices sunlight glinting off the twelve-year-old's dirty-blonde hair. She looks at the ground and notices the stems and leaves from yesterday's weeding lying shriveled in the brown dirt.

And then again she hears a sound from the forest across the pasture. Finally, always too late, she realizes that something really is wrong. Finally, always too late, she says, quietly yet firmly, "Robin, inside."

Always the response: "When I finish this row."

"Now."

"Just a minute."

A moment's inattention. In the battle between composure and panic, so often indecision wins out, spurred by a strange desire to appear calm when everything inside wants out, and everything outside is falling apart. The desire to remain asleep, comfortable, warm, hidden safely from what you know. A belief that if only you can remain steadfast in the dailiness of your activities, your world will never collapse. And so again Malia pushes aside the sounds, stoops to pick up a basket at her feet. She tells herself not to run, not to let even herself know anything is wrong.

She straightens, and hears another sound, then more silence. At last she understands, and in so understanding realizes the unforgivable stupidity of having ignored the warnings for so long. She starts to shout, "Run, Robin! Run!"

But the words never come. They are always too late. There is a shot, or

part one

silence, and an explosion of blood, red on the dirty-blonde back of Robin's head.

Always in the dream the basket falls, slowly, and Malia runs, slowly, for the house. Gunshots. So slow she can almost see the bullets. More shots, like fireflies in the distant forest. Closer, Robin lies in the brown dirt, the back of her head gone, her skull open, jagged like a broken glass.

The doorframe splinters from gunfire. Bullets whine above her head.

Into the house. And then the voices. Always the voices. Her parents, Dujuan, Dennis, Simon, Ray-Ray, and now Robin. "Run," they say, "Run." More gunshots. Men approaching. Room to room she runs in this dream, each room smaller than the last, until she squeezes into rooms the size of coffins, rooms the size of desk drawers, rooms the size of matchboxes. She hides from the men, hears the gunshots behind her, and always the voice of Robin, "Run, Malia, run."

The dreams. A moment's inattention. A single moment.

Dear Anthony,

I hardly know where to begin. Would "I miss you" be appropriate? After all these years, finally I write. After everything that's happened, somehow it seems unfair for me to suddenly reappear in your life, especially when our contact will necessarily be one way. I can write to you, but you, for obvious reasons, can't write back.

I hope you remember our relationship as fondly as I do, focusing not so much on its ending—which at the time seemed unbearably tempestuous to me, but now seems little more than a summer breeze—as on the time that made up its heart. Our relationship. It wasn't my longest, but it remains my dearest, and by a long stretch my most passionate.

I hope that after all this time you can still decipher my handwriting. For that matter I hope you're still living at the same place. I went to the library and looked you up on the Internet. Your address was the same. I'm glad for that, because that way I can picture you there, and I can picture us.

I can see you right now. You just walked to the corner to get the mail. It's hot, and already the tall grasses are turning yellow and brown. Leggy sweet clovers cascade with blossoms, and the vetch has just started to add its purple to the riot. It's dry. You kick up traces of dust with each step, and gravel rolls beneath your feet. As you walk, you don't look at the first neighbor on the left, because you never much cared for him. He never liked you either (or me, if you remember), so today when he sees you coming he busies himself a shade too quickly under his hood, fiddling with the carburetor so the two of you don't have to acknowledge each other. I remember these things. I remember so much about our time together. Little things, like this.

I guess the kids in the next house down don't play foursquare anymore, unless something has gone very wrong developmentally. Most likely they've graduated to basketball and football. Or maybe by now they've graduated altogether, and don't live there anymore.

The dogs are with you of course. Two. They were puppies then, and now they must be very old. Surely they're walking more sedately than before, maybe arthritically. I hope they've not died. One way or another there's been too much death these last few years. Theirs would add too much to the weight.

You reach the mailbox. A strange envelope. A typed address, and no return. You check the stamp: yes, first class, so it's not junk mail. The postmark. You stop and stand in the middle of the street, wondering who the hell you know in Odessa, Texas.

Well, no one now. I'm mailing this on my way out of town. I'm sure you understand why I can't say where. I'll let you know when I'm ready to leave the next place. Several months ago I moved here, on the run from the latest—and worst—of the deaths. I needed some relief. The first day I asked a woman at a restaurant, "What do people do for fun in Odessa?" She said, "They move away." I've saved a little money, so it's time for me to go.

You don't know how long I've wanted to write you, or come visit you. My family is all dead now. All of them. I don't have anyone *anymore.*

And I really don't have you. I did once, and I feel stupid for giving you away. I know that's not how I saw it at the time, nor maybe how you see it now, yet that's how I see it. But even that isn't so simple. If we'd stayed together I don't know if I would have followed this path, and despite it all, I'm not sure any other path would have been appropriate.

I don't know why I'm writing. It's stupid and dangerous. Yes I do. I need to talk. God, you don't know how I need to talk, and despite our problems we always knew how to listen to each other. But once again it's not so simple. It wasn't just our listening that was so beautiful about our conversations; it was our back and forth. Do you remember that night at the top of the stairs in the public library, interpreting each other's dreams, then describing the sexual play we each had in store for the other when we got home, only to learn to our horror that the stairs formed an echo chamber for the stacks? Knowing that everyone in the library had heard the details of your dream about the hermaphroditic tadpoles and the sixty-foot clam went a long way toward explaining the looks we got on the way out, though not quite so far, I'm sure, as the by-then-general knowledge that I was no longer wearing panties. And there was that time you got the book on the White Rose Society, and we stayed up all night talking about German resistance to Hitler. Do you remember? What was the name of that girl who was beheaded with her brother for distributing anti-Nazi literature? Sophia, I think. Isn't it too much that the Nazis beheaded a woman whose name means wisdom? I remember how beautiful she looked in that black and white photo. Those conversations are why I'm writing to you now, not just because we listen to each other, but because we hear, we understand, we mostly agree, and as happened so many nights, we anticipate each other.

I'm tired, and I want to come home. I can't, so this is as close as I can get.

If you are still friends with Charlie and the gang, please give them all a hug for me, especially Charlie. Of course do not tell them it's from me. I wish I could deliver it in person. And I wish I could give you a hug. I miss you.

I love you. I always have.

Malia

~

Dear Anthony,

I'm on the road. Mississippi. I've never seen so much red dirt. Red dust, red clay, red soil packed hard as concrete. Everything's hot as hell, unbelievably hot, the sort of heat that makes you forget you've ever been cool, that there's ever been any other way to be except sweating, dripping, wilting hot. So hot I hold out my arms so they won't touch my sides.

I'm in a cafe. It has red bench seats, most of which show more duct tape than naugahyde. It's strange how sweat makes these seats simultaneously slick and sticky.

The woman who runs the place is sweet. She brought me a menu, and told me the lunch special: baked ham with real mashed potatoes. I ordered it. No ham, she said. So I said fried chicken. None till tonight. Soup. Same answer. Finally I asked what they did have, and she said she'd go check. I told her it didn't matter: surprise me. She was gone a long time, and when she returned she brought this amazing meat loaf that had a trace of mustard and a smidge of pineapple. And enough mashed potatoes that even you would have been full. Now she's brought a piece of homemade peach pie. I'm too stuffed to jump, but I can't walk away from something like that, so here I sit, writing to you and waiting for the food to settle.

I've been thinking about how and where to start telling you about everything that's happened. You could say it started because one night I stayed downtown too late and got mugged coming home from work. Chance. Wrong place at the wrong time. But women are mugged and worse constantly, yet rarely does that lead to . . . What do I call it? Murder? Terrorism? Stupidity? Brilliance? One of the only sane things an environmentalist has ever done?

So where do I start? My parents? The muggers' parents? Why don't I cut to the chase and go all the way back to Columbus landing in America and the Indians not slitting his throat? How different would things look today if they had resolutely killed all who came to conquer? Would eels still slide up the rivers of the Atlantic seaboard, would passenger pigeons still fly overhead? People often say they wish they could go back in time, and this go-round do it differently. Is that true culturally as well? Do I, too, want to go back and kill Columbus, and those who came after?

I don't like any of this. This theorizing about beginnings is all too abstract, and doesn't do me any good. It doesn't do anybody any good. In any case it's much too complicated. The images and memories swirl around me like so many streamers, like heavy fog in the wind, and when I try to pick out one point of origin, I find it connected to all the others.

Where does that leave me? It leaves me still not sure where to start telling you this story, yet just as sure I need to tell it. It leaves me entirely in the dark as to how it will end. It leaves me hot and full and facing a plate of peach pie that has to be tasted to be believed. It leaves me, to be honest, wishing I could go home, that I had a home where I could go. It leaves me, as everything seems to these days, too near tears for my own comfort.

I need to finish this pie and get out of here. I'll write you again soon.

All my love,

Malia

~

Perhaps the story begins, as so many stories do, with water. Perhaps it begins with a stream, and perhaps it begins with a little girl spending summer days as long as lifetimes playing near this stream, getting wet, getting muddy, and when she gets tired, sitting on the banks to listen in on conversations between trees and frogs, grasses and water. Always water. Perhaps it begins with evenings overflowing with the sounds of crickets and early mornings heavy with fog. Perhaps it begins with this little girl watching water condense in tiny drops on leaves, then watching these drops join others to drip off the ends and into the stream.

Or perhaps it begins much later, still with water. Perhaps it begins with a river.

The river was not always this way. Once the river was full of fish: shad, river herring, sea lamprey, sturgeon, eel, trout, striped bass, salmon. The Atlantic salmon, long as an arm, swam seemingly with one goal in mind, to come home, where they would spawn. The fish—so many they kept you awake at night with the flapping of their tails against the water, so many that people were afraid to launch their boats for fear the fish would capsize them by their numbers alone—hurled themselves up waterfalls, and failing to make the top, hurled themselves again and again until through force of will they made it, battered, bleeding, exhausted, home. Now the salmon are gone. So are the bass, the eel, the sturgeon, the lamprey, the river herring, the shad. A few trout hang on, but not so well.

Once, you could drink the water. Once, there were no signs posted telling people not to eat the fish, no signs telling them not to swim in the river. That, too, has changed.

Perhaps this story starts with Malia sitting by this river. She comes to this spot often, because just right now, just right here, in the early evening sun, feeling against her skin the warmth the stones have stored through the afternoon, she can almost forget. Here she can pretend there is no city, no poison, no cancer, no dying children. Here she can pretend the fish still swim, only deep, where she can't see them.

She watches a dozen swallows dance over the surface, twisting and climbing and diving so suddenly that her breath comes in catches of surprise. In front of her, thin stems of willows quiver in the current. Some move slowly, in rhythm with the river's waves.

Others resonate with a different frequency, responding to a pulse she can't see.

Quick movement makes her look again to the swallows, and she follows one as he beat his wings, coasts, then flutters out of sight behind a pine downed in last winter's flooding.

Life, she thinks. It's not so fragile as sometimes we fear. We all want so much to live. The downed pine's branches point upward, and the light green of this year's growth shows the tree hasn't given up. Its torn roots still clutch at the soil, and its branches still reach toward the sky. It still produces cones, the next generation's attempt to carry on.

Once, an amusement park covered the far bank. That was long ago. Almost no sign of it remains, at least at this distance. Malia wonders how long it will take for the same to be true of the city as a whole. She hopes within her lifetime.

A pair of mallards wing their way from her right to her left, and she barely hears the whistling of their wingtips above the roll and whisper of the river.

She's been coming here for years, ever since she went to work for the Council Against Toxics—or CAT as they sometimes call it, or more often just the Council—but each time she comes, it's harder to go back.

It's getting late, though, and she has work to do, and she can't stay here forever, not this time.

Still she sits. A gnat lands on her hand. She looks closely, careful not to breathe. So tiny, the gnat could be crushed even by an accidental exhale. It opens and closes its wings slowly, and she reconsiders her position on the fragility of life. Life is supple and tenuous, she thinks, evanescent and tangible.

The gnat leaves, and she inhales deeply of a sweetness that takes her home. Childhood. Backyard. Picnics. Her parents. A locust tree. Climbing. A treehouse filled with the scent of locust.

The smell reminds her of her niece, Robin. Eight years old. Conceived under a locust tree out back at her parents' farm. Malia's sister Helene had brought a boyfriend up for the weekend, and they slipped away in the middle of the afternoon. Robin. She was named after the locust tree, *Robinia pseudacacia*, so that no matter where she went, she could take the tree with her. Helene died, and Malia and her parents raised Robin as their own. Malia has no children—she's never wanted to bring a child into an industrialized, overpopulated world—and so loves Robin all the more, fiercely, like a daughter.

Time passes, and still she sits. Even in the growing dark of early evening she can see a small school of minnows in the shallows at her feet, and to the side a scuttling crawfish. *It's all so unfair*, she thinks, *so damned unfair*.

It is this recognition, or rather remembrance, of the fundamental unfairness of what is being done to the river and to the people who live nearby that finally gives her the will to stand, stretch, and begin the long walk back to the office.

She follows a steep path away from the river. At the top of the slope she's back in the city. In front of her stands a tall brick building, its windows dark holes that have long since lost their panes. To her right a parking lot abuts another building.

She looks to the fronts and tops of several nearby buildings. Everywhere, she sees razor wire, barbed wire, bars on windows. Whole fronts of buildings sealed off with iron or steel. How odd, she thinks: these fortifications have become so much a part of our lives that we generally forget they're here. An alien dropped unprepared into the city would think we've all gone mad, or that it had landed in a war zone. It would probably be right on both counts.

Dear Anthony,
    I don't know what it is about me and food lately. A few hours ago I went to a barbecue joint in Memphis. I walked to the counter

and gave my order. The woman, an African American, said, "You're taking this to go, right?"

I said, "I'm not sure."

She said, "No, you're taking this to go," and looked past me into the room.

I looked over my shoulder, and realized I was the only white person there. Of course that by itself wouldn't have mattered at all; what did is that everyone else had stopped eating to stare. I told her I'd take it to go.

So now I sit next to the Tennessee River, at Shiloh. Shiloh means place of peace. Most of the trees along the river and through the park—beautiful huge oaks, chestnuts, and loblolly pines—are younger than a hundred and forty years, but I keep thinking about how the oldest of these trees were nourished on the blood and flesh and bone of the people who died here during the Civil War. I think, Someone died right here, or Somebody took a bullet in the leg over there. All these men's lives changing each in a single moment on those April days.

This all ties back to my obsession lately with beginnings. How did I get started on the path that's brought me to this point? And once started on this path, could I at any point have turned back? Would I have wanted to?

Here's what I'm getting at: Once you've committed yourself to a path—or, as often happens, once someone else has committed for you—how do you find new options? I'm wondering not only about myself but about these others as well: I don't believe the deaths here, for example, were just bad luck: soldier A happened to step into the path of bullet B. Sure, luck had something to do with it, but if you put yourself in the position of charging toward a mass of men all shooting at you, getting hit hardly qualifies as an accident. So when did the paths start? With fathers raising patriotic sons? Earlier? By the same token, where do the stories stop? Maybe the stories even of the dead aren't over yet. I look at the green fields and the dark hollows, and at the flat spaces of the mass graves, and I think about the people left behind to mourn the dead, and I think again about the trees nourished by these men's bodies. Every story that ends ripples out to affect every other story. Is there then no *ending, really, or beginning? I don't know.*

Between the last paragraph and this one I put down the pen and looked at the river in front of me. It's huge and muddy and beautiful. I've been trying to figure out what subject I've been dancing around in this letter, and here it is: immediately after that first killing—the only killing I'm directly responsible for, no matter what you may have heard—nothing happened. I woke up two days later—I never did sleep that first night—pretty much the same as before. Ten fingers, ten toes. I was surprised I hadn't been struck down by lightning. The question I faced was: How could I reconcile now being a murderer with being the same person I'd been two days before?

I can imagine how the newspapers would respond to this confession: they'd probably call me a sociopath. But that's not what I'm saying. I'm saying that something had changed in the world—and in me—but that I remained fundamentally the same person I had been before. Only different.

Does this make sense to you? I wish I could see your face when you read this, and I wish I could know your response. It scares me to write it to you. By now I don't care so much what anyone else thinks, but I do care what you think. These past couple of years my secret wish has been that you may not have believed what has been written of me, and not only that, but that you may actually be proud of me, of what I've done and who I've become, or maybe who I've been all along.

I need to close this letter now, and mail it off. It scares me too much. If I don't mail it now I will tear it up, burn it, and throw the ashes into the river. I will write again soon. I promise.

Love,

Malia

~

Or perhaps the story begins with someone else, with a young man named Dujuan sitting with his mother in a doctor's office, listening to the doctor—the white doctor—talk about

Dujuan's little sister. "Sometimes," the doctor is saying, "in advanced cases of leukemia, parts of the blood necessary for clotting are lost. Bleeding occurs more easily." The doctor tells them that his little sister, his mother's youngest child, had bled into her brain. Dujuan's mother grasps Dujuan's hand so tight her fingertips turn from brown to burgundy as the doctor describes Shameka's skull filling with blood, her brain being forced through the only open space, near the spinal column. "She suffered no pain," the doctor says, "because she was fully unconscious." And then he says, "All things considered, not a bad way to go."

In this moment, sitting across from the doctor in the doctor's office, Dujuan wants to kill him. Dujuan sees himself stand, sees himself pull out his knife, sees himself lean across the doctor's desk, sees himself cut the doctor's throat. Perhaps first, he thinks, he should knock the man unconscious, so he will feel no pain. Then he could say to the doctor's family—the white doctor's family—"All things considered, not a bad way to go."

But he doesn't move. He sits there and looks at his mother's face, brown, beautiful, tired. He continues to hold her hand. He holds onto the outrage as well, directed not so much, after that initial rush, at the doctor, who is the messenger, as at the death, and especially at how it happened.

He'd been there when she died, actually seen the life go out of her body, out of *her*. He hated that image of her body taut, every muscle straining as if to tear her apart, her eyes rolled back in her head, and then the convulsions, the rhythmic flailing of her arms and the arching of her back. A primitive groaning had emerged from her throat.

Dujuan had yelled when her body went rigid. That was when the doctors and nurses came. They'd pulled him from the room so they could work on her. But before they took him out, he saw her one last time, her body seizing. This was not his sister. Not any longer. She was gone.

The worst part for Dujuan, except, of course, for the death itself, was that she knew. All along Shameka had known she was going to die. Soon.

She had only cried about it once. Dujuan remembers a night about two months before she died. He'd gotten up about one in the morning, and walking by the room Shameka had shared with their sister, he'd heard her crying. He had stopped, stood, listened. He had wanted to go in and hold her, but hadn't known what to say, what to do. So he hadn't gone inside.

Since that night Dujuan has known that if he could do one thing differently it would be that night, and if he could change one thing about her death it would have been to make it so she didn't know, and didn't have to be afraid. He would have made it so she went out suddenly, like a light switch. *Nobody deserves to die afraid*, he thinks. *Nobody*.

Or perhaps it starts with a planning commission meeting, with five commissioners—five white commissioners—sitting on a stage, four feet of vertical space and a long desk—and of course power—separating them from the people—a few white, most black, some Mexican, some Vietnamese, a few Hmong and Filipino—who step up to a microphone and use their timed ninety seconds to beg the commissioners not to do what everyone here knows the commissioners are going to do. Malia gets her ninety seconds. So does her co-worker Dennis. So do others. So do the people who live—and die—near the river. After each ninety seconds a timer sounds, and if the person continues to speak, the microphone is cut off after another ten. Only four people are allowed to speak longer, and no one is surprised at who they are: a Vexcorp attorney who uses big words to state that a denial by the planning commission of this chemical refinery's expansion would be illegal and would certainly lead to lawsuits; a Vexcorp economist who uses big words to detail how the multiplier effect will raise the standard of living for everyone in the area; a Vexcorp scientist who uses big words to make clear the stupidity and even arrogance of those who attempt to link Vexcorp's effluents, minimal as they may be, to local cancers, which his own studies have shown time and again to be no higher than normal anyway; and Vexcorp's owner and CEO, Larry Gordon, who uses simple language so that simple people can understand how much he cares for the community.

The next day the newspaper will run an article emphasizing the sharp split in public opinion about the expansion of the Vexcorp chemical refinery. To illustrate this split the reporter will quote each of the men associated with the corporation—the only four people who testified in favor of the expansion—and then balance these four quotes by choosing two from among the sixty locals who spoke in opposition.

Only those who have never before attended any meetings like this—and especially only those who have absolutely no experience with the entire political system—are surprised when the commissioners vote five to zero in favor of the expansion. The others know that fifty thousand could have testified against, and so long as those four testified in favor, the expansion would take place.

This is democracy as we know it.

⊕

Of course the story doesn't really begin at that meeting, which was merely about the refinery's *expansion*. It didn't even start fifty years before, with a similar planning commission meeting where people similarly opposed the refinery's construction, and were similarly ignored.

The truth is that there are as many starting points as there are atrocities committed by this culture. In other words, there are a lot of starting points, both distant and proximate. If we really want to go to the starting point, we need to go to the start of this culture.

But what if we use this as a starting point for the story? The Gordon family fortune began in paradox, in the blood-red days of early American history. By all accounts Miles Gordon, the progenitor of the fortune, was a good man. He was a Christian. He did not beat his wife. He did not beat his children. He did not beat his horses or cattle, and once intervened to stop a neighbor from beating to death an exhausted mule. He did not drink strong spirits. He rarely smoked. He did not read novels. He did not dance. He spoke out, to whomever would listen, against slavery. He attempted, when possible, to Christianize the savages who crossed his path. When this was not possible, when Indians attacked or did not keep their bargains by staying off his land, he was swift in retribution and swifter afterward in forgiveness, allowing the vanquished to live so long as they removed themselves from this new land he had, as he recorded each time in his diary, "justly won by the sword in defensive warfare." By 1790, his fortieth year, he had thus justly won some quarter million acres of forest, much of it so dense with cedar, chestnut, elm, and heart pine he doubted the soil had seen the sun since God created the world. Thus he became one of America's richest settlers, which meant one of its most respected.

Miles Gordon passed on his virtues and his land to his children, who multiplied them both, until by 1830 the family controlled an abolitionist newspaper, a bank, an insurance company, a mining company, a chemical company, and a good portion of both the state and federal legislatures. That was the year the family bought controlling interest in Northeast Transport, a company that shipped cotton—planted, raised, harvested, and processed by slaves—to all parts of the globe.

The paradoxicality of the Gordons' position—that without businessmen like them, slavery would never have been possible—never occurred to them, just as Miles's paradoxicality regarding his own amassing of wealth had never occurred to him. Why should it? They did nothing wrong.

But their ignorance went beyond mere willfulness. It was a gift. For as well as having been given a gift for acquiring money, the Gordons had been given an even greater gift: a lack of imagination. It was no more possible for them to see the connections between

their wealth and the poverty, enslavement, murder, or disposses-
sion of others on which it was based than it was for them to see the
backs of their own heads. The Gordons balanced their ledger sheets,
watched their stocks rise and fall and rise again, increased their
inventory, and paid their bills. Life was simple, and guided by two
tenets: use your gifts, and take care of your family.

During the Civil War the Gordons speculated in US
bonds, which rose and fell when the Union won or lost battles.
Lawrence Gordon installed a telegraph wire in his office over which
he personally received up-to-the-minute accounts from General
Grant's private telegrapher. He often knew results of battles before
President Lincoln did. The Battle of the Wilderness, with about
50,000 casualties, netted him a cool million. He made a quarter
million off Cold Harbor, where those who died had pinned their
names and addresses to their shirts before the battle. His son,
Joseph Gordon III, never had to pin his name to his shirt. Early in
the war his father had written to him, in a letter that crystallized
both of the family's gifts, "In time you will understand and believe
that a man may be a patriot without risking his own life or sacrific-
ing his health. There are plenty of other lives less valuable." Soon
after, young Joseph developed fainting spells.

The family gifts did not end with the Civil War. Strike-
breaking, land fraud, child labor: through the nineteenth and twen-
tieth centuries, if there was money to be made, the Gordons were
there. This was not to say the Gordons had no conscience, nor even
that their collective conscience had been erased by money, power,
or any other strong anesthetic, because to do so would be to suggest
that on some level the Gordons perceived their actions as wrong.
They did not. Just as increased prosperity for slaveowners meant
better living conditions for slaves, and just as a certain amount of
control over slaveholder profits provided the Gordons with lever-
age to ameliorate the worst of slaveholder excesses—both of which
were, after all, the real reasons the Gordons entered the lucrative
business of transporting cotton—so too all of the Gordon family's
economic activities were ultimately beneficial to all concerned, if

only one had the right perspective. And the Gordons, generation after generation, always had the right perspective. Take child labor. In the late 1870s Joseph Gordon III, who, with the war safely over, no longer suffered fainting spells, commented, "The most beautiful sight that we see is the child at labor. As early as he may be set at labor the more beautiful, the more useful does his life get to be." Thus did the Gordons share their gifts.

The family continued to share these gifts by investing in armaments during the First World War, German ball-bearing plants in World War II, and oil exploration in South America and Nigeria in the 1980s and 1990s. And, of course, by investing in chemical refineries in American inner cities.

Larry Gordon IV, CEO and primary owner of Vexcorp, is by all accounts a good man. He is a Christian. He loves his wife and dotes on his children. He has never struck anyone in anger. He does not drink. He does not smoke. He is an outspoken advocate of affirmative action, and his companies were among the first to offer full benefits to the partners of homosexual employees. He contributes heavily to both the Sierra Club and Audubon. He is liked by nearly all who know him, and lionized by many who don't. Larry Gordon is a good man.

Larry Gordon enjoys playing with his children. Scrabble, Yahtzee, Chinese Checkers, you name it. He often plays Concentration with his five-year-old son, Terry. They pop popcorn, set up a card table, and lay out the cards. Terry carries phone books from the kitchen to place on a chair, then takes his spot opposite his father. He has an uncommonly good memory, and as the game progresses he effortlessly begins to pluck pairs of red queens and black sevens from the table between them. He perches on the phone books, hands folded on the table in front of him, then moves one chubby hand to the fourth row, fifth column to pick a card, and with a sly smile leans to choose its match. The family—competition is a family pursuit—applauds whenever Terry wins.

Gordon never lets his children win. He never lets anyone beat him. With those not close to him it is because he enjoys—enjoys is too weak a word; lives for—winning. With his children his motivation is different: he wants them to know that when they win it is for real, that he has given them no advantage. He enjoys watching them crow and preen when they beat him, and even encourages them to brag, so long as their bragging is deserved.

He often contrasts that—not aloud to them, but to himself and to his wife, Barbara—with his own early experiences of winning. He'd been precocious, like Terry, like all his children, and had often beaten his older siblings at games of their choosing, from monopoly to cribbage to, much later, poker, played never at the time for money, but for matchsticks, marbles, or most often, their father's poker chips. He still remembers them saying, nearly each time he beat them, "We let you win," and he still remembers his sudden fury that always followed these unexpected deflations. Since then, and of course he couldn't have articulated this at the time, he has insisted on eliminating any possibility that his own victories—or those of his children, whom he loves as himself—could be deflated. His, and their, victories must be complete.

None of this means that his competitions with his children are hard-edged. The games are fun and relaxing: within the family, this necessity for total victory is more undercurrent than obvious, and the simple truth is that both he and his children enjoy their time together. Each child has his or her favorite game. With Terry it's Concentration. Janet, fifteen, loves basketball. Stewart, eleven, is a fiend for baseball, and for elaborate statistical simulations he plays with buddies flung worldwide across the Internet. Tracey, his twelve-year-old daughter, is a wiz at chess. She beats him maybe a third of the time now. That's significant, for he's been playing since his father taught him some forty years ago, and is very good. There's rarely a time when the chess board isn't set up in the family room, on the granite in front of the downstairs fireplace. They both sit on the floor, leaning against the hearth. Summer evenings the cold stone feels good against his bare arms as he waits for her to make her move. He loves watching her concentrate, and loves seeing the unselfconsciousness of her focus: lips pursed, right index finger tapping gently at the edge of the board, half-shut eyes moving their gaze slowly from piece to piece before she'll suddenly close them completely to help herself think. He loses himself in these details, not just of her, but of all his children, and of his wife. Especially in these moments, Larry Gordon becomes aware of how fortunate he is, to be living the life he's created, surrounded by the family he's made, loving them and being loved, knowing that tomorrow they will still be there, and the day after, and the day after that.

Dear Anthony,

I've been surprised by how many people have recognized me. I guess that's not the surprise, what with me now being a star of sorts on programs like America's Most Wanted. *The thing that is surprising is that nearly all of the people who've recognized me have wanted to help. They've seen beneath the media lies to the real story, which is a story they too have experienced on one level or another, and they've told me they wish they had the courage and the opportunity to do the same. I always tell them they must have mistaken me for someone else. They wink and say they understand, and some have given me money. There have been times when I have taken this money. There have been times when I have needed it. There was a woman who let me stay at her home, no questions asked, for several weeks. I know that sounds risky for each of us in our own way, but it was evidently a chance she was willing to take, some way she thought she could help, and as for me, I've had to develop a strong sense of whom I can or cannot trust. There have been times when all it took for me to leave a town was a semi-concealed second or third glance by someone at a grocery store or gas station. Suddenly I know I'm blown and little else matters besides getting away and covering my tracks.*

I've changed my hair color a few times, my hairstyle often, and of course I've frequently changed my style of dress. Still, at least once in a while I get recognized.

You might be asking yourself why I haven't just left the country. We so often hear of people who've committed serious crimes who are then caught a month later three blocks from the scene of the crime. Before all this I always wondered why they didn't just move to Venezuela.

I think for me there've been several reasons. At first my parents were still alive, and we were able to see each other a few times. It tore us apart to only have those furtive meetings, but they were far better than nothing. And then of course when we all knew they were going to die we met so I could take Robin with me. I know the press has said horrible things about me raising her on the run, but all four of us— most especially Robin—wanted us to stay together. We thought it would be best. Of course we had no way of knowing they would kill her. No way at all. Had we known . . .

Another reason I haven't fled the country is that this is my home. I feel like we—all of us, every living being—have been on the run from this culture ever since it started. And nowadays we—so many of us Americans—are on the run from this insane corporate state that is thrashing around killing everything. I now see much of my activism prior to the night everything changed as a continuation of that running away, even though I didn't entirely see it that way at the time. And that one night did change everything. Everything.

Yes, I'm still running. No, I'm not yet accomplishing anything. Yes, it would be safer for me to run to Cuba or Venezuela. But I can't help thinking that there's a reason for me to stay, that there is more I can accomplish here. I just have to learn or discover or remember what it is.

I'm going to sign off for now. I hope you are having a wonderful day.

Love,

Malia

Dear Anthony,

Now you receive an oversized postcard from me! Every USPS employee from here to there can read it! But that's good, because I finally figured out where—or at least with what—this story starts. I can't believe it's taken me this long—years, really—to name the thread that holds it all together, the thread without which there is nothing. The thread of course is love. It all starts with love. And of course it also starts with love's opposite, which was never hate, but emptiness. I'm excited!

To Malia, this is the most beautiful place on earth. It is where she grew up. In the front, the land slopes gently away from the farm house toward the sugar maples, and beyond them an orchard, where the limbs of ancient apple trees have already begun to bow under the weight of their fruit, swaying in the slight breeze that threatens to break up the heat. The apples are early, but even the earliest are not yet ripe. Beneath the trees, flies and yellow jackets buzz above the browning grasses, searching for fruits that have fallen or been thrown by the trees, and that now lie rotting on the ground. Further down the slope is a pond surrounded by cattails, each stalk sprouting a blackbird with red and yellow ensigns on his wings.

Early in the spring the pond was alive with the sounds of frogs, and later, tadpoles swam the sun-warmed shallows. Now the tadpoles are gone, turned into frogs who have disappeared into meadows and forests.

The land crests behind the house, then begins to fall away. Just beyond the crest stands a barn, old when Malia was born, and old, too, at the birth of her father. The barn is tall, and part of it is open, with shafts of light from holes high in the walls and ceiling that highlight motes of hay-dust and sometimes tiny birds who fly among the rafters and call softly to each other. Malia played here often as a child, and sometimes now plays here with Robin.

In one corner of the barn is a large room where early each

August the family extracts honey from the several hundred hives they have at drop sites scattered across the county.

Her father is different from many beekeepers—even those who, like her father, do it not fulltime, but as a sideline to their main farming (in her father's case dairy)—in that he doesn't believe in renting his bees to migratory beekeepers who take the hives crop to crop. He doesn't like the way all that moving tears apart the equipment, but far more important, he doesn't want any of the bees to die so far from home. He always maintains this, even in the face of the incredulity many people openly express on hearing it. He says, "Moving them that far just confuses and scares them."

"But what about the money?" they nearly always ask.

He responds, "Any farmer who's in this for the money is a goddamn fool."

That is one thing among many that Malia has always loved about Anthony: when he visited to help with the extraction one year he did not ask why her father never migrated. He understood immediately the toll that would take upon the bees.

Malia's father always extracts honey early, figuring that if the bees give him the excess of what they bring in during June and July, he should let them keep everything they bring in from August on. Consequently most of the hives go into winter with 150 pounds of honey or more, and even in these days of heavy losses from mites and pesticides, most of his hives emerge each spring bubbling with bees, ready to throw swarms or bring in an excess by May.

Each year in early August Malia takes off work to help with the extracting. She's up there now, working with her parents and with Robin, who uncaps honeycombs by scraping a fork across their surfaces. Robin does this as well as anyone. For a time when Malia was a little girl, they had used an electrically heated knife to cut away the cappings, but one year the knife had stopped working, and in desperation they had tried a simple kitchen fork. They'd found this low-tech solution much quicker, easier, and less damaging to the honeycombs, and so had adopted it. Every year her father retells the story of this failed technology.

Malia's job is to ride the extractor, a big galvanized cylinder with a metal frame inside that spins on ball bearings. She puts uncapped honeycombs into the frame, and starts an electric motor attached to a simple clutch she releases slowly to allow the frame to build up speed—not too quickly, so as not to cause the honeycombs to collapse under their own weight. The spinning frame hurls honey against the inner wall of the tub. The machine is bolted to a sturdy table, which in turn is bolted to the floor, but because it's impossible to distribute the honeycomb's weight perfectly evenly, Malia sits atop a tall chair, knees spread and pressed tight against the metal to keep the machine from wobbling too much. She's long-since become an expert at running the extractor, and now breaks few honeycombs.

A few moments after she begins to release the clutch, the first drop of honey plops to the inner surface of the tub and sticks, a pencil-eraser-sized globule of honey and wax. Then another, and another, until the surface is covered and a mist fills the interior of the tub, even drifting above to leave a light spray across her face and the front of her shirt. The tub's walls become thick with honey, which pools at the bottom and flows out a spigot at the machine's base into a five-gallon bucket. When the bucket half-fills they replace it and pour the honey through a pair of panty hose stretched over a settling tank. The hose expand—become legs of honey that ooze beads of viscous sweat through the fabric—and filter out the wax and dead bees that remained in the honeycombs and were flung to the side of the extractor. After settling, the honey is poured into thousands of scavenged jars and sold.

Boxes of honeycomb can be heavy, so her father does all the lifting, carrying full boxes to Robin to be uncapped, emptying the bucket, and moving empty boxes back outside.

Her mother has always helped with every task, and in addition kept the family well-supplied with food, from sandwiches to fruit to full meals. When the family does other chores she makes plate after plate of cinnamon rolls as well, but because the typical response to honey on your fingers is to lick it off—and of course there's honey everywhere—no one, not even Robin, has much stomach for sweets during the honey harvest.

This year her mother is dragging. Malia doesn't know what it is. Maybe a virus. But this has gone on longer than most bugs. For months now Malia has been watching a slow slide as her mother loses energy and weight. Not a lot, but enough that Malia notices, and she is sure her father does as well.

Malia suspects cancer. But Malia always suspects cancer. She never can get a handle on whether her job has sensitized her to it, or if it really is everywhere. Two of their neighbors have died of it. Pesticides seem to kill as many farmers now as machinery, and as many as suicide. It's not inconceivable that cancer could reach even to the farm. Her parents are organic from way back, as her grandparents had been, back when everyone was organic, before the Second World War. But cropdusters often overfly the farm on their way to or from some other destination. And Lord only knows what sorts of chemicals have made their way into the aquifer.

To Simon, *this* is the most beautiful place. Not because it's beautiful, but because of what he feels right now, and what he knows he'll soon feel, and not feel.

A streetlight flickers and dies above his head as he leaves the sidewalk. He feels the hard dirt beneath his shoes, and in the near-dark sees the tendrils of dead and dying grass that spiderweb their way across what at one time must have been a lawn. He's been here often enough, and often enough in the daytime, to watch his step for the pieces of stone-dry dog shit that lie scattered where they're thrown on the rare occasions anybody bothers to clean the cages out back.

He looks again to the street—a hollow gesture since he's already checked a half-dozen times, and also since, as he thinks, even if cops were to raid the place right now, before he even made the door, he'd still be hauled off for possession of paraphernalia, curfew violation, or some other shit—and sees it's still empty. Then he looks again, and once more. There's an empty car down the street in front of him, but is it really empty? *You're being stupid*, he thinks, but he checks the street one more time. No cops.

He'd biked down here, and chained the bike to a power pole a couple of blocks away. That wasn't for fear of cops, but of crackheads. The bike is nice: he still can't believe he found it in the trash outside a dorm the day the university let out in the spring. Everyone he knows trolls the U-District after the students leave, but none of them has ever heard of someone scoring a $500 mountain bike, much less keeping it to ride instead of selling it. But it's his.

He makes his way across the darkened yard to the first step of the sagging porch. That's when the anticipation really hits him. The slight buzz he's felt till now becomes an electricity running over his whole body. His mouth gets dry, and already he can taste the crack. Already he can feel it down the back of his throat, down his arms and legs, in his balls, up his back. The hair on the back of his neck stands, and he feels pimples rise on his arms. He walks up the steps, hesitates, then raps on the door.

No one answers, so he knocks again. Still no answer. He tries it. Locked. Raps again. Finally a woman answers the door. Simon recognizes her. It's her house. She lets people party here. Meth's her thing. She has dark circles under her eyes, and open sores across her forehead and along her left cheek. She's wearing rubber gloves, and has a broom in one hand.

Simon says, "Red Dog around?"

"Come in, Simon. I'll get him."

He steps in. She closes the door behind him, points him to the living room, and without another word walks to the back of the house. The house's familiar smells welcome him: dirt, old sweat, stale tobacco smoke, piss, old sex, and the faintest car exhaust smell of an active crack pipe.

It's dark inside, though not so dark as outside. He turns into the living room, which is illumined only by a single bare bulb in the next room, the kitchen. The carpet is worn, and where it's bright enough to see colors, a faded green. In the far right corner of the living room is a rotting orange sofa, on which sprawl a man and woman. The man stares at Simon as though trying to puzzle together who or what he is. The woman leans against the back of the couch. Simon can't tell if her eyes are open. She wears a medium-length skirt, bunched up to her thighs. Her panties—or at least Simon assumes they're hers—are on the floor near her feet. The light isn't good enough for him to be able to see between her legs. Next to the panties is a rig.

He's seen these two before. Heroin addicts. He looks again between the woman's legs.

The man says, slowly, in a subdued voice, "Sit. Chill."

Simon can't tell if the man on the couch is trying to communicate with him or with a figment of his own imagination. He looks around, perches on the edge of a cushionless wooden frame that probably used to belong to a dining set.

"Chill," the man repeats.

Simon puts a little more weight on the chair, feels the frame shift ominously, and wonders why he's obeying a junkie. He stands, looks around, thinks about trying to find Red Dog. He remembers the great time he had in this room just a few days ago, and begins to wonder if there's anything left, anything to fill his craving till Red Dog shows up.

Nah, he thinks, not a chance any leftovers would make it through two days on the carpet in this house. But still he tries. He looks near his feet, then toward the light in the next room, eyes darting back and forth. Then he spies some. Score! His stomach jumps as he reaches down. Fuck! It's a fucking piece of petrified cheese cracker. That's not going to do him shit. He's starting to itch. He focuses. Somebody's got to have dropped some. He can't find any. His eyes fall again on the cheese cracker. He forces his eyes away, searching desperately for other anomalies to inspect. But he can't stop himself from looking at the crumb. Is it a cheese cracker? Simon looks closer. Damn, it is. Or something like a cheese cracker. But there's a chance, just a chance . . .

Simon pulls out his glass piece, spotless from two days of scraping for extra residue, and carefully but impatiently places the piece of cheese cracker in on top of the chore. He's about to begin melting it to the side when he hears footfalls moving quickly toward him from behind. He doesn't even have time to turn before he finds himself wrapped tightly in someone's arms.

⊕

Janey, Malia's mother, looks at her husband's hands. She loves Fred's long fingers. No matter how he works, no matter how the skin of his knuckles cracks from cold, no matter the chipped and shattered fingernails he gets from working on machinery, his hands remain slender and soft to her. And strong. She has seen him pick up a bathroom scale, put his fingers around the edge and squeeze, running the dial all the way around. They've been married going on forty years now, and she still loves the feel of those hands on her body.

She walks up behind him to where he stands next to Robin, helping her with the uncapping, and puts her hands gently on his sides, resting them just below his rib cage, fingertips on the seams of his shirt. She feels him shift ever-so-slightly to acknowledge her touch.

Janey sees Malia reach to turn off the extractor. The sound of the machine dulls from a roar to a metallic hiss, and then to the sound of bearings rolling inside their greased cup.

The extractor stops. Normally there is no conversation when the extractor runs, because it's too loud. Necessary communications are either shouted or gestured. Then when the machine stops there is always a long or short silence as each person slowly emerges from the comforting trance of repetitive work. This time Malia is the first to speak. She says, "I heard Hobarts lost their farm."

No one says anything. The only sounds are those of Fred pulling frames of honeycomb from the hiveboxes, and the soft sound of Robin scraping away the cappings. Janey steps to a bench and sits down. She would not exactly say that she is tired, but she does not feel energetic enough even to stand.

Fred says, "That makes four this summer, doesn't it?"

"Five, honey," Janey says.

"I always forget the Cunninghams."

"Didn't he. . . ?" Malia starts.

"Nobody knows," Fred says. "But everybody's pretty sure it wasn't an accident."

No one speaks.

Fred continues, "Even the adjustor is pretty sure, but he's doing what he can to get Edna the money."

More silence.

Finally, Robin says, "Do you think it hurt when he crawled into the bailer?"

Still more silence before Fred answers, "I can't see how it would have taken more than a few seconds."

Janey loves how Fred always takes Robin seriously. And of course she does the same herself. That was how they had raised their own children, and that was how they were raising Robin, she doubly their own, first through birth to their daughter Helene, and second through adoption at Helene's death.

Fred continues, "If it was an accident, there was probably a moment of panic, and then he was too surprised to feel much. If it wasn't an accident I hope he was drunk."

Malia asks, "He did drink, didn't he?"

"Toward the end, yeah."

Robin asks, "Would you do that?"

He turns to look at her. He says, "No." Then he touches her shoulder.

Malia asks, "What would you do if you lost the farm?"

"I don't know. I guess we'd sponge off our daughter."

Malia smiles before becoming again suddenly serious. She asks, "Why do you think Cunningham killed himself?"

"Insurance money."

"No, I mean why did he turn it in instead of out?"

Janey watches Fred flick at the rough table in front of him with his thumbnail. Finally he says, "Maybe he didn't know who else to blame . . ."

By now Malia has begun to unload the extractor, putting the empty frames into hive boxes for her father to carry outside. There the bees will lick the sticky honeycombs clean. Then Fred will put away the boxes for the winter, sealed against mice and wax moths.

Malia catches her mother's eye. "You all right, Mom?"

Janey nods. She feels useless right now. She isn't accustomed to this lack of energy. Every day of this marriage she's been up to cook breakfast with Fred, and she often spends the day working at his side. When the day is done she cooks the evening meal. Helene had been born here at home in the midst of a tremendous snowstorm. When the contractions began, Fred had driven to get Doc Hansen. They—Fred and the doc—had gotten stuck on the way back, and been forced to walk the last several miles. Meanwhile Janey'd had the baby, and presuming the men would be hungry when they arrived, she'd cooked them dinner. That was nothing extraordinary. It was simply her way. It was how her mother had been, and her mother before her. She has not been to the doctor for her current fatigue because they have no insurance, and because every day she hopes she will feel better when she wakes up. But every day she feels a little more tired.

Now Malia is reloading the extractor, spinning its frame by hand to put a heavy comb here, a light one there, balancing it out. She works quickly, and soon it is full. She turns it on and slowly releases the clutch. The machine gains speed.

Janey looks at her daughter, wind from the spinning extractor blowing back her hair, and feels for her a love every bit as strong, every bit as passionate, every bit as painful, as her love for her husband. Malia worries her. No, more than that. She frightens her. She's not worried that Malia will do anyone harm, but that harm will come to her. She knows her daughter well enough to know what she is thinking as the frames spin round and round:

she is thinking about Cunningham turning his anger inward, not outward, and she is thinking about what it would have taken to convince him to do otherwise.

✦

"Simon. Just the man I want to see." Red Dog—called that because one of his first dogs, a pit bull long-since dead, had been auburn with black markings—releases his bear hug.

Simon pulls crumpled bills out of the front pocket of his pants.

Red Dog says, "You read my mind. You see, I'm in a bit of a cash-flow crunch . . ."

Red Dog puts his arm around Simon's shoulder, and Simon doesn't know whether he should feel threatened. Red Dog is compact but strong. Simon has seen him do a dozen hand-stand pushups, lower his body to the right and to the left, parallel to the ground, then bring his body back up for another dozen pushups. He'd gained this strength in prison, daily doing hundreds and then thousands of burpees in his cell and dips on the yard.

Simon sees Red Dog smile, his mouth full of rotten teeth. Red Dog pulls him away from the other room into the hall, flattens out Simon's bills, says, rapid fire, "Six dollars? You brought six fuckin dollars? Get the fuck down to the 7-11 and buy yo-self a box of M&M's and a fuckin Slurpee."

"C'mon, Red. Don't do this. You know I'll make it up to you."

Red Dog just looks at him.

Simon says, "I swear, man."

"Damn, motherfucker. You always beg. Always a fuckin dollar short and about two weeks late."

"But I always bring you your bread, don't I?"

Red Dog just stares at him.

"Every fuckin time, Red."

Red Dog says, "Look, you already got my balls in a wringer. I can't keep fronting you this shit. Hell, I can't even keep fronting myself."

Simon wrinkles his forehead.

Red Dog says, "I tell you what, though. You ever hear of twelve-fifteen? Belushi special? I got one rigged up and ready to go."

Before Simon can say he doesn't like needles, Red Dog is talking fast, "Man, I just got some from that bitch down the hallway. She introduced me. This shit is A-one. I'm talkin straight up off the chain. Better than that rock, even. And it's cheap, man. Answers all of yo problems. Fuck, it's the answer to mine. You get more mileage for yo money. And there's no fucking crash afterwards."

Red Dog starts patting Simon on the shoulder, fast and hard, until Simon feels like he's being burped. Red Dog's rattling so fast Simon's ears began to ring. Simon grins; he's never seen anyone so fucking pumped.

"Hey, tell you what. Come in, I've got a, you're not gonna fuckin believe this. Come on. Come on." Red Dog keeps tapping him on the back, and begins to herd him down the hall. His mouth won't stop rattling.

Simon begins to laugh. He has a taste at the back of his mouth and he hasn't even gotten there yet.

Red Dog runs the forefinger of his free hand along the base of his nose, and sniffles. He says, "And it only costs you twelve bucks. You got another six bucks? Everybody's got twelve bucks. Even fuckin panhandlers got twelve bucks."

Simon holds out his hands.

Red Dog looks at them. "Shit, you don't even have twelve bucks. What the fuck you spend your money on? You been buyin handjobs again down on East Colfax?"

"I never did."

"Course not, and nobody ever did you, neither." He stops, then says, "I tell you what. You always been good for it. Six now, and ten next time before you even think about asking me for anything else."

"Yeah, I'll do it."

Red Dog smiles, says, "No more buying handjobs, though. Gotta save your money for next time."

Simon grins, thinks about bantering back a "Fuck you" but he's too excited now to say a word. Red Dog says it's better than crack. Simon can't believe that. Nothing's better than crack. Crack is everything. Crack tells him he's all right, that he's better than all right, that he's the one and only, that he's perfect as he is, that there is no problem he can't fix. Every time he takes that first hit, when he hears the scream of that aluminum train rushing down the tracks toward his brain, racing down the tunnels of his ears, thundering into his body, consuming and covering him, he knows, even just for that so-brief time, that he is invincible. He can do anything. He can be anyone. The world is his.

But this won't be crack. Finally, he says, "This will be good?"

"No," Red Dog says. "It's better than good."

It is late. Malia has gone to bed to read. Robin is long-since asleep. Janey feels Fred's weight on his side of the bed, and his heat, but not his skin. She thinks about Malia, and her hair blowing back in the wind of the extractor. She thinks about Malia's question, about the turning inside of anger, and asks Fred, "If we lost our farm, what would you do?"

Fred is silent long enough that she thinks he might have fallen asleep. But finally he says, "I wouldn't kill myself."

"I know." More silence, and then she says, "But thank you for saying that."

And then he says, "I wouldn't go down without a fight."

She thinks about his words, and then asks, "What does that mean?"

He says quickly, "I don't know what it means." Then he adds more slowly, choosing each word carefully, "It means I was born here, and I know the patterns here. And I don't ever want to leave. If I had to leave, it would be like losing part of me. Like if I lost you."

She searches for his hand beneath the covers. She says, "Are you ever afraid?"

"It used to be never," he says. "But now? Every goddamned day. Every goddamned day."

Dujuan climbs the fire escape to the rooftop. He loves coming here at night, especially hot summer nights when he can almost feel the tomatoes and peppers stretching out their leaves, like hands reaching out to hold him. He walks across the gravel, and can feel the heat rise up to his ankles and bare calves. He sits in one of the folding chairs next to the boxes of dirt and green.

When he was a kid he used to come up here and sit with Montrell. Montrell—everybody calls him Boo—used to make him read all the goddamn books on gardening. Dujuan had hated that at first—all his friends used to tell him gardening was gay—but had done it because his brother told him to. Now he's glad he did.

He'd smoked his first joint here, too, also compliments of Boo.

Earlier this year, he'd sat up here with Shameka. By then she'd been too sick for him to pass on the tradition of the first blunt, but she'd not been too sick for him to introduce her to gardening. So in the spring they'd come up as soon as the ice was gone and put in seeds for peas, lettuce, carrots, radishes. He hated radishes, but hadn't known how long she would live, so made sure to plant some. She'd clapped her hands when they'd poked above the soil. Later they planted beans and tomatoes and peppers they'd started in her room next to the radiator.

Far in the distance he hears a siren, which changes its pattern, changes it again, then stops.

The garden is doing well, though not so well as last year's. The beans are a bust. But the squashes are threatening to take over the building. Runners dangle over the side, and he fantasizes about reaching out his window to pluck a zucchini. He loves zucchini for its toughness—nobody messes with a zucchini, and it thrives on whatever shit you dish it out—and for its aggressiveness. Today the rooftop, tomorrow the fuckin world.

He loves the smell of the garden, the smell of dirt mixed with the pungent smell of nightshades, the strong scent of mustard, and the way all this mixes with the smells of the city—asphalt, gas, the greasy smell of Mrs. Ballinger frying chicken.

He wonders where Simon is, and what Ray-Ray is doing. He hasn't seen them today. The three normally spend at least part of every day together. They've been friends since before Dujuan can remember.

Dujuan wishes the rooftop were higher, farther from the brightness of the streetlights, overlooking the whole city. He wants to see it all laid out before him like a map.

But then again, he thinks as a light goes on in a third floor bedroom across the street, sometimes the view here isn't so bad. A couple of times over the years he's seen Mrs. Jasper undress, and once he saw her and Mr. Jasper have sex. But most of the time, like tonight, she drops the shade. And then he wishes again he was way up high, where he could see it all.

Red Dog is right. The speedball is better than crack. The speedball is better than everything. After the release of the belt buckle on his bicep, after the prick of the needle, after the cold metallic taste of coke, comes a rush of warm dizziness, of energy, up his arm and into his brain, moving out from there to the tips of his fingers, to the bottoms of his feet, and moving out from there until he feels it penetrating the walls of the building and exploding. He feels himself clenching his jaw muscles tighter and tighter, harder and harder, pushing his front teeth top against bottom, clenching and unclenching until he feels a tiny chip fly off. He's got so much energy. The clenching shifts to the back of his mouth, to the molars. Every muscle in his body is clenching. A single tear squeezes itself out of the corner of his eye and slides down the side of his cheek. His heart is thundering in his ears. His tongue feels the jagged edge where the chip flew off his front tooth, but it doesn't matter. He is invincible. He's never had so much energy, and each time he thinks the energy can't get more intense, it does. God damn, he thinks, I'm Superman.

But this is too much. He realizes he'd been given too much. He needs to get to water. That's what he needs. He stands, muscles clenching, and he begins to vomit.

He vomits until there is nothing left, and then he vomits some more, and then more after that. He cannot stop vomiting.

And finally he does.

The drug throws images at him, rapid fire, each one forgotten as soon as the next begins to appear, each one forgotten before it can even register. His mother. A broken window. A little kid in a blue ski jacket. A dog with three legs. He's hot. He's so hot. Hot like he's standing in the snow without a jacket, sweating from standing still. The feeling is too intense, too strong, too quick for him to grasp it. And the aluminum train is back, louder than ever. It's a fucking freight train, rushing straight toward him. The images fall like rain. His mother again. A high heeled shoe. His mother coming out of her bedroom, behind her a man. Then another man. Another. A broken television set. His heart is beating faster and faster, until his ears are exploding again and again and again. Windshield wipers, speeding back and forth.

Simon is standing now. Red Dog is making him drink something. He feels powder in the water, tastes the bitterness. The images still rush at him. An empty Burger King bag. A dead pigeon. The images rush through his bloodstream, and he can't stop the train. It's louder and louder. His heartbeat is faster and faster. He sees himself as a child, sitting alone on a couch.

Simon is scared.

And then something shifts, like that moment on a hot August afternoon when the pavement still burns but you know the day will get no hotter, the moment it starts to cool. The images begin to slow. His muscles start to unclench. He has nothing left, as though his nerves have all been fried.

His heartbeat slows.

His jaws not only unclench, they relax. His whole body not only unclenches, it relaxes.

Time passes, or seems to. He's not sure.

The images slow, become richer. No longer do they assault him. Instead they fill him with emptiness. His mother walks slowly, now, out of her bedroom. She looks so tired. She always looks so tired. Simon is tired, too. Everything is moving slower and slower. An old broom on a sidewalk. A stuffed animal in a dumpster. What did Simon's father look like? He doesn't remember. He never knew him. Never wanted kids, they say.

He's blind. Maybe his eyes are closed. Maybe he is dead.

Images crawl. Simon has a son. He doesn't know him. He doesn't know if he has a son. The son's mother said she was pregnant, and then she disappeared. He never saw her again. He sees his son laughing.

Simon needs water. He wonders if he is going to die. Does he need water? Does he need his mother? His father? He feels the thought: *Someone love me.*

He doesn't blame his father. Who could do it, what with having to get two jobs and all? Simon says out loud, to Red Dog, "I wanna see him laugh." He doesn't know whether Red Dog hears him.

Simon's chest is very tight. He's having trouble catching his breath. He's having trouble getting enough air. His chest is so tight.

Water. It's raining. He feels Red Dog's hands on him. Not that way. A pounding on his chest. A shower. A bathtub. He is in a tub of cool water. Not too cold. This goes on forever. And then longer than that. Finally he says, or thinks he says, "What the fuck?"

Somewhere behind the water and images and the bathtub he hears Red Dog say, voice muffled, slowly becoming more clear, ". . . vicodin in water, didn't have no valium, brought you back, but then pushed you over the other fucking edge. I thought you were . . . I overrigged you. Sorry. Loaded you up heavy. Been doing this all week, myself, and forgot you haven't. It was my rig. You're all right. You're all right. I don't have no fuckin dead body on my hands." Red Dog rattles and rattles.

Simon tries to laugh, but all he can do is whimper. His clothes are wet. He is wearing his clothes. He isn't dead. He doesn't remember.

Dear Anthony,

Immediately after the first murder, things stayed fine. Nobody talked. Our lives continued. Dennis, my coworker, was more brittle and spoke to me a little less, but until the whole thing broke and he killed himself I never was sure how much he remembered, not only because he was drunk that night, but also because he always had a stronger capacity for denial than most of us.

I've seen Dujuan and Ray-Ray a fair amount in the intervening years. They told me that drugs undid us. They told me about Simon, about the drugs, and about Simon talking to people he shouldn't have.

That brings me back to the question I've been asking about beginnings, only this time slightly differently. If Simon hadn't used drugs, would we have gotten away with it? If Simon had used drugs but hadn't talked, would Robin still be alive? If Simon had talked to someone less eager to collect the reward, would Simon still be spending the rest of his life in prison?

There are probably thousands of lessons here, but I've learned two hard ones. The first is to know whom I'm working with. If I were to choose three people from a thousand on whom my life would depend, in retrospect I'd put Simon somewhere between one thousand and, oh, one thousand. The second, and of course I'm violating this with these letters, is that if I'm going to fight back against the full power of the state, I need to keep my mouth shut about it.

I'll write more later.

Love,

Malia

Malia sits at her desk, working. She is in her office at the Council. The Council occupies a suite of five rooms plus a central lobby on the first floor of an old building near the river.

part two

Her walls are bare except for two posters. The first is of Che Guevara, with the quote, "Let me say, at the risk of seeming ridiculous, that the true revolutionary is guided by great feelings of love." The second is a blown-up photograph of a grizzly sow standing on all fours in a meadow.

She hears the door to her office open, and by the time she spins in her chair to face the entry, Dennis is halfway across the room. He reaches for one of the room's other chairs, a sturdy padded roller with thick wooden arms, and drops into it. He leans forward, eyes bright, and says, "Guess what?"

"What?"

"It's on."

She hesitates. "What?"

He looks around, then eyes her closely. "We got bugs?"

"What?"

"Bugs. We got any?"

Malia finally understands. "We're clean."

"Good, because we just scored a huge victory."

"What happened? Did you blow up Vexcorp headquarters?"

"No, really. I just got the call . . ." He stops abruptly, then says, "Don't say that, there might be bugs."

"I swept last week," she says. "Besides, what the hell do we do that's gonna scare the feds?"

"Vexcorp's my worry."

"Same difference," she says. "What's the story?"

Dennis, in his late thirties, began working as CAT's attorney a few years after Malia began there. About six feet, with dark hair, he's handsome in a clean-cut, energetic sort of way. Too handsome, Malia often thinks, or at least too attentive to his looks. Or perhaps just too theatrical. Malia has frequently seen him pause outside windows at restaurants for one final check before smoothing his hair and making his entrance.

Dennis says, "Guess."

"Shit, Dennis. Come on."

He pauses a moment, then says, "*60 Minutes* is going to do a segment."

"No!"

"This story is so sexy," he says. "It's got everything. Poisoned kids—" He interrupts himself, says, "—Poisoned *poor* kids—" He interrupts himself again, "—poisoned poor *inner city* kids, bought politicians, cancer rates through the roof, the fucking river's probably gonna catch fire like the Cuyahoga back in—"

She talks over him, asks, "How much time did they give you?"

Dennis keeps talking: "God, wouldn't it be great if it caught fire when the film crew was here? I can just see it. And we can juxtapose their denials with that handwritten cost-benefit analysis—"

She interrupts again: "—I need to take a look at that—"

Again he continues, "—showing it was cheaper to . . ." He trails off, says, "What? They said about fifteen minutes."

"Is that enough?"

His voice quickens again. "Enough? We're talking 60 Fucking Minutes. The roving eye of American attention is gonna fall on Vexcorp, and the company is gonna feel the heat." He pauses, then says more slowly, "Fifteen minutes is enough. Besides, any more and people would get bored."

He stands and begins to pace. He says, "If enough people just know what's going on . . ."

"They do know, Dennis."

"But now it'll be undeniable. Pictures. Right there. TV's stamp of approval."

This is the hope, Malia thinks, that allows every activist to go forward: the belief that if only people could be given the right information, they would do the right thing. Malia long ago concluded this hope is essentially false. She says, "People either don't care or they don't know what to do."

"We'll tell them what to do."

"Write their fucking Congressman?" This is a sore point with Malia. The solutions presented by environmentalists, including her office-mates, including herself, are never sufficient to the problems. Getting poisoned by toxic effluents? Write to the head of the company requesting it change its practices. Democracy not functioning? Write your Senator begging him to not follow the money. She continues, "That guy doesn't take a dump without Vexcorp's OK."

Dennis stops pacing.

Malia stands. She asks, "Or maybe they should write letters to the editor. Of the corporate newspaper. Or maybe they should call the local TV channel. I read Vexcorp's board is interlocked with Viacom."

"Don't start."

"I also read Viacom holds four million shares of Vexcorp."

Dennis glares. "Just don't fucking start already."

More weary than angry, she says, "Viacom owns CBS."

He begins to pace again. "Can't you let me have five minutes before you start? Things are bad enough without your hardline bullshit." He stops, turns to face her, says, "People get turned off by your doom and gloom. They want happy. That's what sells."

"Like poisoned kids and a dead river?"

Patient, as though talking to a child, he says, "That's the great thing about this *60 Minutes* gig. I have an angle."

They stare at each other.

Finally, "Aren't you going to ask?"

"Of course, I'm just waiting for you to tell me."

"Jobs," Dennis says.

They stare at each other again. Malia is not going to ask what he means. She is not going to ask what he means. She is not going to ask what he means.

Having built up the suspense, he volunteers, "Vexcorp's going to clean up the river—"

"Shit," Malia says under her breath.

He continues, "—in one of those public/private

partnerships. I heard Cash is going to introduce a bill—"

She interrupts, "Great name for a Senator."

He laughs. "There *is* a God."

"*And* She's got a sense of humor."

Dennis says, "Anyway, a source told me he's going to announce the bill's introduction tonight at a fundraiser."

She stares into space, then looks at him sharply, says, "Let's go."

Silence.

"To the fundraiser."

"Get serious."

"I am."

"I don't think you understand. It's a fundraiser. It costs fifteen hundred dollars just to sit down."

"Then we'll stand. We can make up some papers to look like a subpoena, or we can make a citizen's arrest for treason."

"Are you crazy?"

"We'll figure out something on the way."

Dennis takes a deep breath, then continues as though she hadn't spoken, "The unemployment rate in this slum is above fifty percent—"

Malia interrupts softly: "—Dennis—"

"—and this is going to create over 400 jobs."

"Let's go."

He says, "The feds are going to provide the money."

"To Vexcorp, of course."

Dennis asks, sincerely, "What do you care who gets the subsidy, so long as the cancer rate goes down and the river gets clean?"

"You've been doing this too long to believe this bullshit."

"That's where *60 Minutes* comes in. We publicize the hell out of it, and Vexcorp can't back out."

"They won't back out. They'll just take the money and do nothing."

He shakes his head. "When are you going to learn you can't

always fight them head on?"

She looks away, then back to him before she says, "You know, we've never even tried that."

He stares, blinks twice, slowly.

She knows she lost him. She continues, "We push paper around. They're not scared of us."

"You bet they are. Why do you think they plant bugs?"

"They're bored, paranoid. How would I know?"

"They plant bugs because we're effective," he says. "Just last year do you remember the legislation—"

"—Eviscerated in committee, and turned into an industry initiative by Cash . . ."

"It almost worked."

"That's one reason we always lose," she says. "We consider our losses near-wins."

"We got the message out. Right now that's what matters."

"No. Stopping the poisoning is what matters." She doesn't want to be having this conversation. She may as well be talking to an answering machine. Press one to hear *We must never be emotional.* Press two to hear *We must present only reasonable demands.* Press three to hear *Our tactics must fall within bounds declared acceptable by those on the other side.* Press four to hear *We must not call the other side "the other side" because the language is too divisive.*

She wonders if Dennis, too, feels unheard. Perhaps he does. She sees clearly that in order for him to keep at the work, Dennis has to focus on one particular task. When he maintains that focus, he's effective at achieving his goals. Whether the goals themselves accomplish anything is an open question. Malia sometimes wonders, too, if what she perceives as seeing the system clearly for what it is—a maze with no exits—in actuality is a way to allow her, too, to keep working. Perhaps she is as wedded to lost causes as Dennis is to superficial productivity.

Dennis shakes his head in a way that signals the topic closed. "This is a win-win situation. Vexcorp wants money. They get it. We want a cleanup, and we get that."

"No justice."

"Fuck justice. I want a clean river, and I want the kids to stop dying of cancer."

He has a point, if it will work. If.

They're both silent. Finally he says, "You have a special way of puncturing people's balloons, you know that?"

Dennis is right. This isn't the time to have this conversation. Not on the heels of his good news. And Dennis probably isn't the person to have it with. She says, "I'm sorry. Really. What you've done is great. I don't think anybody else could have done it."

He looks at her.

She thinks, *Time to mend some fences.* She says, "I sure as hell couldn't have pulled it off."

He isn't having it: "I don't know."

"No, absolutely. You're a genius. Brilliant."

He smiles a little, says, "Well . . ."

She asks, "When will they be here?"

"In eight weeks."

Neither speaks for a few moments, before Dennis says, "Say, you want to grab a bite to eat to celebrate?" Another pause, very short, before, "Like old times."

They had dated briefly right after Dennis began working for the Council. For Malia, the relationship had been at that boundary between the forgettable and regrettable: neither bad enough to regret nor good enough to remember or mourn. It seems to her that Dennis felt their relationship more important, in ways she was reasonably sure he couldn't articulate.

She says, "Thanks, not tonight." Then she gestures toward the document on her desk. "Friday's the deadline to appeal this EIS, and I've still got a half-dozen arguments to tear apart. Besides, I should crash the fundraiser."

"Want some help?"

"With the fundraiser?"

He points at the document.

"No thanks," she says. "How about a raincheck on

dinner till next week, and also, can I borrow your Vexcorp files? That's where you've got the copy of that cost/benefit analysis, right?"

"It's on my desk. I'll get it."

Dennis leaves, then returns with a bulging file folder. "You can hang on to it for now. But don't lose it. I'll need that stuff when *60 Minutes* shows."

He turns to go, then turns back and says, "Are you going to be all right here?"

"If I get into trouble I'll yell and the wiretappers will rescue me."

"Don't joke. You gonna be all right walking to the bus?"

"I do it all the time."

"I worry all the time."

"Thanks. I'm a big girl."

Dennis leaves. She turns back to the document on her desk, rubs her eyes with the palms of her hands, and gets to work.

Malia makes her way along the crowded sidewalk. Her skin feels abraded, as though all the eyes are pieces of grit on sandpaper, each one taking a tiny piece of her. But right now she needs the crowd.

She sees that no one is using the payphone she has chosen, in a carrel against a brick wall not far from the stream of people. She stops, removes her backpack, and pulls from it a pre-paid calling card. Then she lifts the receiver and dials the number from the card. She knows from memory the number she is calling. She says, "Hello, Anthony?"

There is a pause before he recognizes her voice. He says, "I'm glad you called."

"I can't talk long."

"I understand."

"How are you?" she asks.

"It's good to hear your voice."

"And yours. Would you have recognized me?"

"Not out of nowhere, no. But after your letters, yes."

She pauses. *"How are the dogs?"*

"Old and happy."

"And the cats?"

"They run my life."

She laughs. *"So nothing's changed."*

He laughs, too, then stops, asks, *"How are you?"*

She doesn't say anything for a long while. The street is loud. The people. The cars. She can barely hear him. She says, *"Do you want me to stop the letters?"*

"No."

She speaks slowly, *"I don't want to make you uncomfortable. Or anyone else. Are you married? Am I intruding?"*

"I don't think you'll upset the cats."

"But what about you? Do they— Are you scared?"

"Of the letters?"

"Of being somehow involved with me . . . Of—"

He cuts her off, laughing, *"Of being involved, period. You should remember that much from our time together."*

"No, not that. Because of my . . ."

"Of course I'm scared of that. I'm scared of everything. I'm a writer, remember? That's why I write instead of act. I'm a professional coward."

"No . . ."

"But," he says excitedly, *"I've been dying to tell you. I dreamt about you the night before I got your first letter. Not only that, but Sophia was in the dream, too . . ."*

"The beautiful girl . . ."

"But in the dream her actions were different. She said, 'I did everything they asked. I sold out my neighbors.' Just then in the dream there was a knock on the door. I went to answer it. You yelled for me to stop, but it was too late, and stormtroopers flooded in."

"What does it mean?"

"It means there's something weird going on with you and my dreams . . ."

She had forgotten the way he runs his words together when he *gets excited. She wishes she could see his face. She pictures him gesturing, using his whole body to speak.*

He's saying, "But it also means it doesn't do any good to sell out your neighbors. And it means be careful." He hesitates, then says, "Are you scared?"

The question brings her back to this busy sidewalk. She says, "Always. That's why I can't talk long."

"I assume you're taking precautions . . ."

"That's why I don't have a cell phone. And now I'm on a crowded street," she says. "Even on a trace I can be lost before anyone gets here."

"Why would my phone . . ."

"Your books."

"They're just words."

She doesn't say anything. Finally, "I'd rather be safe than make more mistakes. I don't want to yell too late again to stop the stormtroopers."

"Again? It was a dream. My dream."

"No, it happened. Not with you. With Robin. I'll tell you another time."

Silence.

She says, "I've got to go for now. I'm nervous about the time. I'll write you soon."

"I would like that."

They say goodbye. She smiles easily, and realizes how unfamiliar that feels. She hangs up the phone, then slips into the stream of people flowing along the sidewalk and makes her way, slowly, cautiously, by a rounded route, back to her car.

"Fuck, it's cold," Simon says. "Whose motherfuckin idea was this?"

The three of them—Simon, Dujuan, and Ray-Ray—lean under the open hood of a car. Ray-Ray occasionally flicks on a small emergency flashlight to look desultorily at the engine, an incomprehensible tangle of steel, wires, and rubber tubing, but for the most part the three just stand, shiver, and wait.

Dujuan says, "You got a better idea, Einstein?"

"I just thought . . ."

"Okay, so it ain't the best fuckin idea I ever had. But it's better than workin for these white folks."

Simon thinks, then says, "If they pay me cash, I'll do whatever the hell they say."

Dujuan replies, "You wanna flip burgers, motherfucker, take yo ass down there and fill out an application."

"Nah," Simon says. "I get a job, it's gonna be at Victoria's Secret."

"You? A model?"

"Nah, asshole," says Simon. "I'd be workin in the back so I could check out yo bitch."

They all laugh. Dujuan says, "You'd have a fuckin peephole in the dressing room . . ."

"Full-length one-way mirror."

"Dream on."

"If you're gonna dream, dream big, dog. That's what my old man always said."

They all laugh again. Still laughing, Ray-Ray says, "Fuck you, Simon. Your father never taught you shit."

A brief silence, while Ray-Ray and Dujuan exchange a glance. Simon begins to talk again, this time too quickly, "I'll bet he don't have to get a fuckin job. I'll bet right now he's—"

Dujuan cuts him off with a quick hand motion. Simon stops and follows Dujuan's gaze to where a car is turning a far corner. The headlights sweep toward them. Ray-Ray turns on the flashlight, and he and Simon look intently under the hood. Dujuan walks into the street and begins to wave his arms. The car slows, and Simon holds his breath. Then the car swerves around Dujuan and speeds away.

"Fuck," Dujuan says. "Maybe this is a stupid-ass idea."

"It wouldn't be so bad," Simon says, "But I'm freezin my ass off here. Feels more like December than March."

When no one responds, Simon feels compelled again to fill up the silence. This time he says, "It's really not such a bad idea, Dujuan. Just bad luck so far. We've just got to wait a little bit longer."

Larry Gordon sees a woman out of the corner of his eye, and turns to look. Even though the distance disallows him from making out her features—she's walking up the long hallway from the back of the hotel—he can see that she's beautiful. The fluidity of her movements—the steadiness of her shoulders, the slight swaying of her hips—reveals a consciousness of and comfort in her own body. She sees him, too, and walks more quickly. At last she gets close enough for him to recognize her face. It's his wife.

Gordon enjoys these rare instances when distance or lighting or a crowded room breaks for just one moment the familiarity of twenty-five years of marriage, and causes him to see Barbara anew, to see her as others must, not as the mother of his children and his life partner, but as a never-before-seen woman as mysterious and fresh as she is beautiful.

She comes close, and he sees her skin is flushed from the cold. She says, "I parked in back. The front's a zoo."

"Big turnout," he says. He quickly kisses her cheek.

As they enter the banquet hall, Gordon becomes acutely aware, as he always does, of the looks Barbara attracts from men and women alike. At least as much as he enjoys her beauty for what it is, as he enjoys a fine painting or photograph, he enjoys seeing respect and envy on the faces of other men who see her. He enjoys seeing their glances pass over her face, then stop to go over it again before dropping to her breasts, then moving down her torso to her hips, still slim after four children, and finally sliding down her legs. He enjoys the fact that they can look, and that they want to look, or more to the point that they cannot help looking, but that she belongs to him.

Women, too, turn to look. Never at him, though he's not unattractive—always at her. He knows this ability to attract attention is her gift. He knows that some women are blessed with beauty, and that some men are blessed with intelligence—women, too, though not so often the type of intelligence necessary for business or politics. He knows that his own gift, equally important, is not for attracting attention but for amassing wealth, and thus power, and for using that power to benefit those around him—his family, community, region, and in the end, country. And just as he knows that his own gifts trickle down to make life better for people everywhere, and as he knows more specifically that his gifts make Barbara's life better, make her more highly valued, more esteemed by her community, so too her gifts enrich him, not only in his own eyes but in the eyes of others who see her, and who see they are together.

They sit. Barbara asks, "Did you ask Al about the expansion?"

Larry smiles. "I was going to surprise you. Approval is guaranteed. We still have to jump through bureaucratic hoops, but the Senator gave his word that nothing will stop it."

"So that inspector . . ."

"Transferred."

"I'm so glad." She smiles, too, and nods, then begins, "And the bill . . ."

"My other surprise . . ."

She waits.

"Tonight Al's going to announce the introduction of the cleanup bill to the Senate."

"The one you wrote?"

"Better. It contains sufficiency language for our expansion eliminating the possibility of lawsuits. He predicts it will fly through. What with crushing that other bill last session, he feels it's the right time to take the offensive."

She takes his hand. He feels a surge of energy run up his

arm. She smiles and squeezes. Gordon pays attention to the texture of Barbara's hand on his, and feels the metal of her wedding band against the back of his hand.

He doesn't think many men in their late forties can say in all truth that they have never even considered being unfaithful to their wives. But early in his life, long before their relationship, he conquered infidelity. He had realized as a teen, and then especially in college, as he moved quickly from girlfriend to girlfriend, that infidelity held a special attraction for him. He loved that first time being led into a woman's bedroom, smelling the scents there in her private room that are more personal than perfume, more personal than her smells of sex, the scents that accumulate day after day and night after night as she lives and breathes and dresses and undresses and sleeps and awakens the next morning. He loved seeing into the little hidden places in their lives, into their choice of keepsakes for the tops of their dressers, the decorations for their walls. And he loved that feeling of first penetration, of newness, of pleasing a woman for the first time and being pleased by her. He had known that if he did not *solve* this problem of infidelity, whatever solve in this case meant, that his eventual marriage—it never occurred to him to never marry—would surely fail. This was not acceptable to him.

At last he came upon a solution: he had to find the perfect woman. Only then, he reasoned, when he had found her, would he never be tempted to find another. If he were sleeping with the most beautiful, witty, supportive woman he could find, he thought, he would never be compelled to stray. Love thus became a problem to be solved, a challenge to be met, little different than the problems he solved and challenges he met in organic chemistry, macroeconomics, or any of his other classes. Later, a few years into his marriage, he realized how simplistic his reasoning had been. But by that time it didn't matter, for it had worked, and his marriage was successful.

✦

This is, in fact, a pretty fucking stupid idea. Not just because the night is cold, and not just because the plan isn't working. Nor does Ray-Ray think it's stupid just because it's forcing him and Dujuan to listen to Simon tell story after story. Ever since Ray-Ray made that crack about Simon's father, Simon hasn't been able to shut up.

Simon is telling them about his visit to his cousin Jake's house the previous December. He says, "Jake's mom has one of those fucking yappy dogs that never shuts up and every time you look away tries to piss on your shoes."

Ray-Ray only half listens, in part because he's heard the story a dozen times, and in part because he's still thinking about what's wrong with tonight's plan. It's too complex, he thinks. *Why the fuck do we need to drive to this rich neighborhood when we coulda just got money the usual way?*

Simon is saying, "Christmas carolers showed up, if you can believe people still do that shit. A bunch of rich white fuckers from some rich white fuckin church up town. I wished they woulda just brought cash."

And even if we were going to come up here, Ray-Ray thinks, we should have just gone into some empty house and cleaned it out, instead of standing here freezing our asses off and drawing attention. Besides, in this neighborhood, who's going to stop for two niggers and a white boy—Simon—in the street? They'd be glad we fuckin broke down. More likely to lynch us than help us.

Simon continues, "Well, the carolers knock, and the moment Jake answers, Little Buddy runs out the door, heads straight for this one guy's leg, grabs on tight, and starts humping." He pauses, then says, "Little Buddy, that's the dog—"

Dujuan says, "We know it's the fuckin dog. You think we so stupid we think that's Jake's dad?"

Ray-Ray returns to the conversation long enough to say, "But with Jake's family, you never know . . ."

Ray-Ray and Dujuan laugh. Simon ignores them and says,

"So this guy's in the back row, hoping nobody'll notice. But he's hoppin on one leg and shakin the other, the whole time singing 'Oh Little Town of Bethlehem.' Little Buddy quits at the end of the song, and runs back in the house just like nothing happened."

And this wasn't the right thing to do, Ray-Ray thinks. He's never had a problem taking money from rich people, because like somebody once told him, behind every fortune lies a crime. And he certainly doesn't mind hitting stores, because most of those fuckers gouge the hell out of everybody (it's a point of pride, however, that none of them has ever so much as shoplifted from Becerra's Grocery, because old man Becerra never hurts anybody), and also because the stores never pay for it themselves: it just comes out of some huge goddamn insurance company. And to rip off an insurance company could never be a sin; it is nothing but a good thing. Sometimes people walking the streets are okay targets, too, because they look down on him, or because he can tell they don't fucking deserve what they have.

Simon says, "He's a love em and leave em kind of dog."

But why this? Somebody was going to stop to help them, and because of that the person would get robbed. Where's the justice? Besides, it's stupid as hell to use Dujuan's car when they don't need to. They stole license plates, but why take this chance?

"Wait," Simon says, "Here's the best part: as the carolers turn to leave, Jake's mom says, with a straight face—"

Dujuan and Ray-Ray interrupt to say in unison, Dujuan far more enthusiastically than Ray-Ray, "Well, Mister, I guess he likes your shoes."

Dujuan bursts out laughing, and finally Simon says, "You've heard that one."

Silence. A car drives by. It doesn't stop. Dujuan doesn't bother to go into the street, and Ray-Ray and Simon don't bother to turn on the light under the hood. Dujuan says, "Well . . ."

"This was crazy," Ray-Ray says.

"That's the point," says Simon. "The dog—"

"Not the dog. The car. This. Tonight."

"Maybe," Dujuan says. But they don't stop waiting.

Ray-Ray is concerned about Dujuan. He's changed since Shameka died. Before then, Ray-Ray had never known anyone so smart, so quick with a read. Dujuan'd always known before trouble happened, and his predictions of trouble were always right. More than once he'd ducked behind a corner or sped from a stoplight moments before someone pulled a gun, or he'd decided not to go someplace because there'd be trouble. Ray-Ray had known Dujuan long enough to not remember a time when Dujuan's ability to avoid unnecessary danger had surprised him. Always it had simply been a part of who he was, like his laugh or his habit of scratching the side of his face when nervous.

But the Dujuan that Ray-Ray knows and follows and even loves is dying. It's not that his predictions have gone bad, for he always still seems to know. It's that he's grown reckless. He's been taking chances he never did before, and he's begun devising plans, like this one, that seem to have no purpose.

And he's become violent. Dujuan has never avoided kicking someone's ass, or telling Ray-Ray to, when it's necessary, but there's always been a reason. Money. Stubbornness. Revenge. Now Dujuan no longer seems in charge of the violence. It's in charge of him. The reasons for violence no longer always make sense. Dujuan no longer makes sense.

Before Ray-Ray's eyes Dujuan is falling apart. His skin is peeling away, and his flesh is coming off the bones in great chunks. Someone else is growing beneath, and Ray-Ray doesn't know what this new Dujuan will look like. Because of that, for the first time in his life, Ray-Ray is scared.

An armed agent stops Malia from entering the banquet hall. His gun isn't obvious, but it's there, evident—and intentionally so—from the small bulge in his jacket, and from the way he holds his arm slightly away from his side.

The place is crawling with agents. Even in this ritzy hotel

the Senator has to be protected. The agents, she thinks, are like the razor wire and iron grating: we accept their presence, and never think about what that presence means.

The agents all seem the same, like Hollywood stereotypes of what government bodyguards should look like: tall, broad Aryans, overgrown frat boys on cocaine, with puffed out chests and nervous-yet-empty eyes, slight swaggers, and the impeccable courtesy of those who know that overwhelming force is on their side.

One of the guards says, "I'm sorry, ma'am, but you can't go in."

"Isn't he my Senator, too?"

"Do you have a ticket?"

"I don't have 1,500 dollars. I just want to ask a question."

"You'll have to make an appointment, ma'am." Another agent comes to assist the first.

"Why do they get to go inside and I don't?" She doesn't want to waste time talking with these agents, and isn't sure why she's continuing. For that matter she isn't sure why she came. Had she expected to be led to a microphone, and for everyone in the room to listen rapt? Had she expected them to take up torches and burn Vexcorp to the ground? She has no idea what she could say— or even if there was *anything* she could say—to reach these people.

"You'll have to go now, ma'am."

This fucking *ma'am* business is getting on her nerves. She begins to move around him, but he steps back and cuts her off. He still hasn't reached to touch her.

From inside the room she hears the Senator talking about the importance of the Vexcorp plant's expansion. It is crucial not just to the city but to the country. It stands for everything American.

The second Aryan asks why she doesn't write the Senator a letter.

She sees a space between the two men, and wonders if getting inside is worth getting arrested. In that split-second of opportunity she plays out in her mind the scenario of disrupting the speech, then getting tackled and removed by the two men, plus three or four of their buddies. This scenario ends with her shouting a line that came to her one night as she fell asleep, "The silencing of dissenting voices has long been the cornerstone of tyranny." But she isn't sure she wants to waste that line on this audience, and in any case thinks the line, which sounds noble in her head, would sound appallingly corny if uttered aloud. So she doesn't move.

The men don't move either. They watch her, casually it seems. But she knows if she makes a fast movement they'll pin her in an instant. She wonders what they're thinking, or if they are thinking at all, and for one brief and delicious moment wonders if they even *can* think. Perhaps they were bioengineered specifically for this job, to have big muscles, quick reflexes, and brains tiny enough to disallow original thought. She wonders if either has ever lost anyone he loves to cancer. And then she wonders if they defend the Senator because they believe in him, or because the job pays reasonably well, or if there are other reasons. Perhaps they're control freaks who believe that an unjust order is preferable to disorder. She wonders if they ever think about the gap that separates those on the inside of the room from those on the outside, and she wonders if they understand the elasticity of this gap: the wider the gap, the more force with which it will eventually implode. If the gap gets wide enough, she thinks, they'll have to bioengineer these guys with consciousness small enough to disallow even primal fear.

"I tell you what," one says. "You give me your message, and I'll make sure the Senator gets it."

The Senator finishes his talk. Those in the room applaud.

"He's taking questions," she says, "Let me ask one from here."

The two men look at each other. She can tell they're inclined not to let her, but can also tell they've not been briefed on this precise possibility. She thinks she knows the answer to the question of original thought.

Had there not been a long moment's hesitation between the Senator's call for questions and that first polite raising of a hand, she never would have said anything. But even before she knows what she'll say she shouts, "Mr. Senator," and begins waving her hands.

Caught in that tension between the possibility of turning a small scene into a big one and hoping it will simply go away, the agents freeze. The Senator, too, perhaps bioengineered from the same stock, slowly raises his hand to point toward her. She can tell he doesn't like her—someone who didn't pay the $1,500 to be in his presence—or more specifically, he doesn't like his sense of her impending deviation from the evening's script, but in the absence of any better idea for how to control her he lets her continue.

Still not knowing what message she'll give, she opens her mouth, and hears her voice say, clearly, "On trial for his life in Jerusalem, Adolph Eichmann said nobody ever told him that what he was doing was wrong."

The Senator looks confused, and slightly pained. She doesn't know what words will come next, but knows she must speak quickly. She feels the bridge between the two worlds—the Senator's and her own—disintegrating beneath her feet. She is aware that cool language will keep the bridge intact slightly longer, but she doesn't know what good soft words over an ephemeral bridge would do. She hears her voice, speaking clearly yet quickly, "I won't allow you that excuse. The Vexcorp expansion is wrong, and it's murder."

The two men grab her. She locks eyes with the Senator, and reads his mind. *In any other country*, he thinks, *I could have you shot. And in any other country, I would do exactly that.* Before the agents can begin to physically move her down the long hall to the rear of the hotel—they don't want her ruining photo ops later in the front lobby—she hears her voice shout, "You'll see me at your trial!"

The last thing she hears is the Senator's response: "That's exactly why the Vexcorp plant needs to expand: so we can make anti-psychotic drugs available to those who need them."

An eruption of laughter from the crowd is followed by applause.

Applause follows her down the hall, and out the door, until

the door slams shut behind her and she hears only the sound of the
freeway in the distance, and her own heart pounding in her ears.

Malia sits near the back of the bus, drained of energy by
the incident at the hotel. It's so tiring, she thinks, to always be the
one who opens the way for others. She wonders what it would be
like to meet someone more radical, more militant than she, so she
could be the follower and not the leader for a while.

She allows herself to be lulled by the bus's rocking.
Through half-open lids she sees and doesn't see other passengers
board or get off. There is an ancient Korean woman in a floral print
dress, clutching a paper sack in both hands. A blind man who sits
by himself. A couple of young men, one black and one white, wearing earphones and listening to music loud enough that she can hear
it, too. Ads blanket the walls, but she doesn't take them in.

She drifts, and in that semiconscious state lets her mind
meander across what she'd gotten done that day. Of course there
was the scene at the hotel. But what had that accomplished? Her
action, she had to admit, had been purely symbolic. The notion of
putting Cash or any of the others on trial is inviting, but who could
create the structure, and where would the tribunal get its power?
There isn't a chance in hell any of this will happen, she thinks,
which means she has to question whether the action was a success
even symbolically. What would these people remember? That they'd
encountered a rude person who attempted to ruin their evening?
That they'd seen an "environmental extremist" face to face? Would
they merely have an exciting anecdote to tell their friends? How
could she make these people feel what she feels? She has, through
her career, tried semi-casual conversation, and she has tried rational
argumentation. She has tried science, logic, and pleas for morality.
She has begged, and she has demanded, and she has realized that
demanding without the power to force change is merely another
form of begging. She has pointed out flaws in logic and errors
in fact. Nothing matters. She doesn't know what will force these

people to stop the poisoning.

What else did she accomplish today? She finished a press release, made headway on an appeal, and started writing a foundation grant report listing last quarter's media hits and, if she was honest with herself, puffing up last quarter's legislative successes, which in reality were nothing more than nominal. In other words, she accomplished no more and no less than what she always does. Did she succeed in helping keep CAT viable as an organization? Absolutely. Did she slow the explosion of cancer? Not on your life.

This is the paradox that defines Malia's emotional response to her own existence, and that holds most of her waking, and dreaming, attention: she has given her heart to her work, yet her work doesn't seem to accomplish what her heart requires. She wants tangible results. She wants for her heart to stop breaking at the deaths of the children, not because she erects barriers around her heart, but because the children stop being killed.

Malia often asks herself whether she hates her life, and what she recently realized is that she feels wildly conflicted. On the one hand she loves who she is. She loves her parents and Robin. She isn't seeing anyone at the moment, and right now she loves being single. She loves doing good work, work that makes a difference. But does she make a difference? It isn't merely that she, one puny person in a big world, is unrealistic in her expectations of what she can accomplish, but more that she's part of a much larger movement that is as ineffectual as she. More and more environmentalists work on more and more toxics issues, and the rates of toxic dumping—and cancer—continue to rise. She used to work on forest issues, and the pattern there was the same; deforestation not only didn't cease, it accelerated. The same is true the world over: when she talks to friends, no matter their issue—biodiversity, ocean health, global warming, anti-genetic engineering, anti-animal cruelty, pro-family farming, economic justice, pro-democracy, anti-corporate, anti-military—conditions are getting worse, and the destruction is accelerating.

The bus slows, and she looks up, and around. The blind

man gets off. Suddenly, and for no reason she can understand, she remembers that the root of the verb to *accomplish* is the same as the root of the word to *complete*. It means to fill up. Perhaps that is her problem. Perhaps there is a dissonance in her own life between what she accomplishes and what she completes. Perhaps she is not filled up. She doesn't know if that is the case, nor does she even know precisely what it means: while in this moment she is sleepy enough to make this connection, she is neither unconscious enough to fully explore it nor awake enough to explain it.

She looks out the left side of the bus, and on a far hill sees the looming tower of St. Luke's Hospital. She counts the lighted rows of windows from bottom to top. The pediatrics ward is five rows up. She visits there often. If she cannot stop the children's deaths, she wants at least to help them through their suffering. She's been in pediatrics wards before, but this one is different. It has the normal collection of broken arms and legs, ear infections, appendicitis, and the occasional accidental ingestion of household chemicals (Malia herself had gone when she was eight to an emergency room after finding a bottle of lemon-scented ammonia: she loved lemonade, and loved the smell of lemons, so she took a deep whiff; her parents took her in when her nose wouldn't stop bleeding). But this ward contains other cases, too. Too many other cases. Bone cancer. Leukemia. Asthma. Systemic lead poisoning. Systemic cadmium poisoning. Systemic this and systemic that.

About a year ago Robin volunteered to start coming with Malia to the hospital every couple of weeks. Malia had been surprised—very pleasantly so—and had become deeply proud of her niece as the visits went on. Robin brought games and toys to help pass the hours—as only another child can—with these kids whose homes consisted now of the four white walls of a hospital room. She played with kids who should be batting balls, but who knew instead the intricacies of IV drip systems. Instead of knowing how to make hayforts, these kids knew how to survive days and nights that dragged endlessly through tests, needles—"just a little stick"— weakness, pain, boredom, and perhaps most of all and finally, the moment-by-moment draining away of their hope.

But a week ago, on the long drive down from the farm, Robin said, "I think this is the last time I want to do this."

Malia's first response, her internal response, had been a flash of anger and resentment. *Why go today then? Why didn't you tell me this before we left the house, before we drove in this car these last two hours? You were the one who suggested this in the first place. Where is your determination? Where is your compassion?* She had stopped herself from saying, *I'm so disappointed.* Instead she had said, in her best there-is-no-judgment-implied-at-all-by-this-question-I-really-just-want-you-to-be-comfortable-and-explore-with-me tone of voice, "Why?"

Robin said, "Because it hurts too much to make friends and then have them die."

Malia nearly drove off the road. She blinked hard to hold back the tears, then pulled slowly to the side.

Robin asked, "Did I say something wrong?"

"No, honey, not at all."

They took a walk. Malia found a side road that led to another side road that led to yet another that dead-ended by a small stream. They walked along the bank, skipped stones at a pond, and several times threatened to push each other in. Finally, Robin had said, "They're expecting us. We need to go at least one more time."

Malia said, "Yes."

And Robin said, "But I don't know about next time."

Malia had replied, "It's okay."

They'd driven on.

The bus stops again, and lets on a large black man with a cane. He greets the bus driver and shakes his hand, then proceeds to make his way back, shaking the hand of everyone along the way. A few on the bus look at him like he's crazy, and a few more look away, but Malia notices that even the most standoffish cannot help but smile. The man seems happy.

Malia remembers sitting next to the pond with Robin, and she remembers wondering, as she often does, what it would be like to live in a world in balance, where she could sit beneath a locust tree—for Robin had searched one out for them to sit beneath—and look to the forests and meadows around her and not have to worry that the trees were dying—as they already were, she could see from the discoloration of the branch tips—from acid rain. She wondered what it would be like to live in a world that is not dying day by day. She corrected herself: being killed. Of all the losses—an intact planet, nontoxic surroundings, cordial relations between humans and the rest of the natural world—she believes that losing a sense of living in peace hurts nearly as much as any. She knows that many people—the vast majority—do not feel this loss, or at least aren't aware of feeling it. She knows that most people are not conscious even of the slipping away of their own lives, passing time in jobs they do not love, in cities they have to shut themselves up against. And if they can't feel even such intimate pains, how can they be expected to perceive these larger losses; if they don't notice the diminution of their own selves, how could they feel the progressive amputation of the rest of the world? Put even more baldly, if they can't raise themselves to outrage over the premature deaths of their own children, precisely when and over what will they ever feel at all?

For Malia there is no choice. She feels what she feels. She doesn't know why this is, but she has always been this way. Walking in the forest, no matter how beautiful that forest may be, she cannot block out the distant whine of chainsaws or forget the silence of absent songbirds. Nevermind the salmon and sturgeon she has never seen, where are the warblers and buntings she heard as a child?

Malia hates that all this is slipping away, and she hates seeing the children bald from chemotherapy. She hates even worse her own impotence in the face of it all. If she can do nothing to slow the momentum, who can?

Suddenly Malia bolts upright. Despite the chill of the evening she becomes hot. She begins to perspire. She wants off the bus. Her throat becomes dry. What if, she thinks with rapidly rising horror, she chose the wrong word? What if the problem isn't that she *can't* do anything, but that she *won't*? What if there are options before her that she cannot, or will not, explore, because the consequences for her own life would, or could, be too severe if she were to choose them?

Perhaps, she thinks as she pushes that internal spotlight off of herself and back to a more comfortable position on others, that is why so many people fail to take sufficient notice of the deaths around them, even the deaths of their own children: perhaps secretly we all see what there is to do, but are afraid to acknowledge it, for fear of what that full acknowledgment would demand of us. We each stand by, she thinks as she notices a single drop of moisture rolling down her side under her blouse, and let the world be killed because we are afraid that if we effectively act, we will each lose our own comfortable positions. Or, if our positions are already uncomfortable, that they will become even moreso.

Malia looks outside. She is having trouble breathing. She reaches up to pull the cord alerting the driver someone wants off. The driver slows the bus. It's her stop.

"This is where I get off," she says to herself, and to no one else in particular.

Later, on the way home, what Dujuan remembers most is how good it felt to finally stop feeling, once the violence began. Until then he'd been edgy, holding down an anger that rose and rose inside of him. He'd snapped at Ray-Ray, and especially Simon, and he'd complained about the cold, but his anger wasn't directed at them. Nor was it directed—specifically—at the man who eventually stopped to see if they needed help, whom they robbed and whom Dujuan beat—shrugging off Simon's and even Ray-Ray's attempts to stop him—more severely than he'd ever beaten anyone. Dujuan knew, even as he heard again and again the thud of his booted foot against the man's ribs, and heard the grunting of the man's involuntary exhalations—the man long since having lost volition—and even as he felt the solidity and *rightness* of the impacts traveling back up his own leg, that he felt no unique anger toward this man as an individual. He didn't know this man, had never seen him before, and would never see him again. He didn't care to know him. He didn't care about this other's pain. What he cared about was how *good*—yet at the same time painful—it felt to feel the texture of the air at the moment the man realized he was in trouble, and to draw out that moment, feeling the other man's fear and tasting his questions, so tangible Dujuan could pluck them out of the air above the man's head: Will I live? Will this hurt? How much will this hurt? Will I humiliate myself in the pain? He cared about the crack in the man's voice, but only because it revealed a crack in the wall that in Dujuan's mind separated the two men. Dujuan accepted his own rage, his own violence, as part of who he was, and as a necessary response to his surroundings. And he somehow knew, as certainly as he knew his sister was dead, that who this man was and what he represented—though Dujuan didn't know what that might be—were based on violence against Dujuan and all he held dear. Dujuan could not have said how this was, but he knew it to be true. And so he beat the man, and continued to beat him.

He stopped when the air turned sour and he knew they had to leave. He hefted the man's shuddering body from in front of their car, dropped the hood, and dashed to the driver's side. He got in and started it up. They had barely pulled away when a police car passed them—presumably a random patrol, or perhaps officers called by the man on a cell phone before he stopped to help—coming the opposite direction.

Dujuan looked in the mirror, and the last thing he saw before he turned down a side road were the headlights of the cop car shining on the man he had just beaten. He did not feel a thing, and for that he was glad.

Larry Gordon is lying in bed, listening to his wife's slow, comfortable breathing. He hears also the distant ticking of a clock—a grandfather clock out in the hallway—and through the window, cracked slightly open, he hears a breeze whispering through the needles of the pine tree in his yard. He turns from his back to his side, and looks out to the brightness of the city sky beneath the eaves. The sky is pale yellow, almost pink.

He can't get comfortable. It's late. He doesn't know what time it is. He turned the digital clock to the wall at 1:15. He isn't particularly anxious. He just can't sleep.

He thinks of that woman from the fundraiser. He knows her well—in an abstract fashion—from his files. She intrigues him, so young and full of righteous indignation. So full of herself and so ignorant of how real change takes place. If she wants to change Vex-corp, he thinks, she should just take a job there, work her way up, and begin to rationally implement whatever policies she can make stick. But of course that's not what she wants.

Gordon catches himself thinking too intently. He needs to stop. His mind is moving too fast, and if he doesn't slow it down, make the thoughts less directed, less precise, less, as a sleep therapist once told him, like a channelized river and more like a muddy delta, he will never fall asleep.

The clock still ticks in the hallway. His wife still sleeps beside him.

He and Barbara no longer have sex. He doesn't know how he feels about that. It used to bother him in the years of its gradual decline. For many years they fought about sex far more than they had it, with his wanting it leading frequently to confrontations that inevitably ended with his feelings hurt and desire snuffed, and often ended simultaneously with her invigorated, sometimes even aroused, by the depth and length of their conversation. He doesn't understand how he and Barbara could present a public picture of such adoration and passion yet in private share so little. Nor does he understand how arguments can engender in her a feeling of intimacy. To him they're simply troublesome. So by now he just accepts their lack of sex, and isn't even sure, if their sexuality were to resume, that he would want to participate. The same intensity of feeling that once had come to him through orgasm comes now from the soft touch of her hand on his arm, and comes even more from nothing she or they do but from the simple security of their relationship, and from his knowledge of her love for him. That's it, he thinks: after all these years it no longer takes the gift of her body to convince him of her love. It simply is.

But he's thinking again. He tries to stop. The clock still ticks. Sometimes at night he hates that sound, each tick reminding him he's not yet asleep, and sometimes—and if he happens to be drifting when this thought comes he instantly awakens—he remembers that each tick takes him that much closer to death. Then he especially hates the clock, and he gets up and physically stops it, to reset it in the morning.

Lately he hasn't liked his dreams, what few of them he can remember. He's never been much good at remembering dreams— he just isn't the dreaming type—and even when he does they're mainly prosaic—a recapitulation of the day's events or in times of especial stress recurring dreams of superficial self-inspection, dreams more horrible than nightmares because they're unrelentingly monotonous, dreams consisting of nothing more than running his consciousness up and down the sheets over his body to make certain the sheets are arranged just so, for if they were to become disarranged, he would . . . He doesn't know what would happen, for the dreams merely continue in their dreary sentinel pacing of his body.

But lately he's had the same dream again and again, and he can neither understand nor shake it. He can't even adequately remember the details: only the terror. He remembers something over his head, and the sound of a door slamming shut. That's it. And the fear. He remembers a suffocating fear that holds him under and forces him to push toward the surface of consciousness till he bursts up in bed, gasping for breath.

Barbara is a sound sleeper, and she never stirs. Each time, he wants to wake her and ask her to hold him. But he never does for fear of being perceived as weak and superstitious enough to be scared by a dream.

He thinks about that dream now, and wonders if he will have it tonight. He wonders if he will even sleep. Sometimes he doesn't, instead just lying there awake, then half-awake, then awake, till dawn, or in the summer till long after dawn, when the alarm clock tells him it's time to start the new day.

Something is wrong in his life. He doesn't know what it is. For the most part he doesn't acknowledge, even to himself, that anything could possibly be wrong. Only on nights like this, and even then only rarely, does this notion—a horrible notion that he does not, cannot, understand—arise. He knows it can't be in his relationship with Barbara, nor with others of his family. And it's not in his relationship with Vexcorp or any of his other companies. He doesn't know what it could be.

For most of the ride home, no one speaks. Nor do they listen to music. The only sounds Ray-Ray hears are the whine of tires; the roar of the car's engine, made louder by a shot muffler; and the intermittent cracking of Simon's knuckles.

Dujuan drives. Ray-Ray looks in the man's wallet. Seventy-five bucks and a couple of credit cards. Split three ways the wages would have been better at McDonald's. Ray-Ray wants to say something to break the silence, but he doesn't know what to say. He looks at Dujuan, out to the passing buildings, then back to Dujuan.

It isn't the violence that disturbs him. He's seen and participated in enough for it to no longer have much of an effect on him. Sometimes he likes it. But he didn't like this.

No one says anything until they reach the apartment building where Ray-Ray lives with his mother. As Ray-Ray and Simon get out of the car—Simon lives a couple of blocks away, and is going to walk—Dujuan says, "I'm just goin drop y'all off, ai'ght?"

Simon says, "That's cool."

Dujuan continues, "Y'all just split it."

Ray-Ray thinks nothing of this last statement until several

hours later, when he awakens with a start and wonders why Dujuan didn't want his portion.

This night Malia dreams of salmon going upstream. The river roars with the flapping of their tails, and is white with froth. Salmon push against each other, and merge to form a larger body, then individuate again to leap at the falls in front of her. Salmon dive deep to build up speed, then leap against the rock wall. Gashes appear in their skin, and blood—maybe only a drop at a time but it fills her whole mind—begins to flow until the river runs red. Again and again they leap, until they make it above to continue their journey home.

In this dream there are people who live with the salmon, and who eat the salmon, and who give gifts to the salmon. She doesn't know what the gifts are, but knows these gifts are as important to the salmon as the salmon are to the people.

Then the people begin to erect barriers against the fish, and begin to sell the salmon to others. There are so many barriers that she can no longer see the river. Malia knows this is wrong, and in the dream, so do the salmon, who continue to leap the barriers both nature and humans place in front of them.

She asks another person, who also sees this commerce as wrong, how the salmon are able to leap the barriers, and he says, "They are angry."

Then Malia's consciousness falls into the river, and is carried along with the fish. When they jump the dams she feels the anger in their bellies and in their spines. When they fight through nets she feels the bite of rope and the deeper bite of anger. As the salmon carry her away, higher and higher in the river, she remembers thinking, "It is anger that will bring them home."

Dujuan sits at his mother's kitchen table, his father's .38 snubnose in front of him. The feelings are coming back. They began to return even before he got out of the car. He can't make them stay away. Sorrow, rage, emptiness, confusion, and most of all an indescribable weight. No longer can he carry his mother, nor his brother and sister. No longer can he carry the memory of Shameka.

He can't run away. Where would he go? How would that help? The feelings would follow close behind. Nothing helps for long. Drugs are useless, because he comes back down. Alcohol is no better because he eventually sobers up. After sex he still has to deal with another person. Sleep doesn't work because he always wakes up, and when the dreams follow him, even there he gets no rest. He had hoped that violence—not just violence used to achieve an end, but violence to which he can give himself up completely—would make the feelings go away, but it did no better than anything else.

He needs to talk to Montrell, to Boo. He doesn't know what to do to make himself feel better, or failing that, to make himself feel nothing at all. Boo would know. Their father would have known. Where is he when Dujuan needs him? Dujuan needs someone, and he knows he can't turn to his mother: he doesn't believe she would know what he's talking about, and in any case she has enough trouble just keeping Shane and Ketheia fed. Shameka's death hit her as hard as it did him.

And she doesn't know how hard he'd been hit, because he couldn't let that show. Had he shown it to her, she would, he was certain, have felt the need to take care of him, something she couldn't do. Not now. Maybe not ever.

He looks at the gun on the table, then watches his hands fumble open the box of ammo and pull out one bullet.

"Chickenshit," he says out loud. He's too damn chickenshit to take responsibility for even this decision.

He breaks out the cylinder.

He would never have done this here if his mom and the kids were home. But they're gone for the week to his grandma's for her birthday. This way his mother will never see the mess. Ray-Ray will check on him tomorrow or the next day, and walk in like he always does. Then he will take care of things. Like he always does.

The table and floor will be cleaned up by the time she gets back.

He inserts the bullet, then sees his hands reach for two more: one in six isn't good enough odds for him.

The sharp snap of the gun fitting back together—which would normally have been barely audible—echoes through the room and through his head. He hears it all down his spine and into the hard wooden chair on which he sits. He hears it in his feet and back up his legs. As he spins the cylinder every click of its ratchet makes its way into his bones.

He sees a hand draw the gun closer to his head. He doesn't know whose hand it is. Shameka's? His father's? Boo's? The man's from the street tonight? He sees tattered skin above one fingernail, then a freckle on the ring finger, and recognizes the hand as his own. He sees the finger squeeze, the hammer pull back. He has not yet reached the point of no return. The finger keeps squeezing. He wants to put the gun down, but can't make the hand do it. He closes his eyes to not see the flash.

It seems there is no one moment when the hammer stops going back and begins to come forward. There is a single smooth movement until the trigger stops resisting his finger and the spring-loaded hammer strikes, with a force weak enough that it could have been stopped by a finger and strong enough to blow apart someone's world.

There is a sense—perhaps even the deepest sense—in which it doesn't matter whether the firing pin strikes a cap or an empty cylinder, because someone is going to die this night, this moment. The only question is whether Dujuan's body will die as well.

Dear Anthony,

I'm sorry I had to get off the phone so quickly. Next time can we talk about you? I'd love to hear whatever you want to say: how you're doing, what you're thinking, what you're working on, anything.

I'm sorry that our communication is so one-sided. I'm sorry I can't give you my address. I'm sorry I can only write when I'm leaving an area. I'm sorry I can't just come over so we could go for a walk.

It's not that I don't trust you. It's the whole damn surveillance state. My fear is that the feds might be intercepting your mail, might be tapping your phone, and that when I'd show up the feds would be waiting for both of us, to nail me for murder and you for harboring a fugitive.

That was one reason I wanted to call. I never asked your permission to write you. I would never want to put you in any uncomfortable position. If this ever gets to be too much, please let me know when we talk.

Another reason I called is that it's been so long since we've seen each other. I don't want you to be some perfect fantasy object, there when I want to talk or need to process but otherwise having no material existence. Frankly that sounds creepy and pornographic to me.

Of course I've purchased and read (and reread) all of the books you've written in the years since we were together—and each passing day makes your analysis of the irredeemability of this entire political and social system ring more true—and I've brought them with me everywhere, even on the run. I lost them all—and lost everything else— when the feds killed Robin. They nearly killed me as well. Afterwards, when my life settled back down a bit, I got more copies of your books so I could have them with me.

But your books aren't you, any more than these letters are me. These letters are a part of me. The lonely part. The hurting part. The part who needs a refuge. And it's not fair for me to put all of that onto you.

part three

But I miss you. Or I miss what I remember of you. Or I miss what I'm projecting on to you.

I keep thinking about that old line about how art is like sex: it's a lot better with two people. The same is true for conversation, for relationship.

I don't want for whatever relationship we have—or if relationship is too strong a word then communication—to be pornographic. I don't want for my letters to be narcissistic, or journal entries. I don't like how the one-sidedness feels, and it's no basis for relationship.

Maybe next time we can talk about whatever you want. That would be fun.

All my love,

Malia

~

Although it's still relatively early, Gordon knows it's going to be another sleepless night, his third in a row. The night before last Gordon stayed up late, in part because he and Barbara made love, their first time in probably six months. He remembers that the last time it had been fall, and just beginning to snow. Now it's spring. After their lovemaking two nights ago, and after Barbara had fallen asleep, he had stared at the dark ceiling, the dark wall, at the bright sky through the window cracked slightly open as always. He'd thought, and not thought, and he had felt empty. He'd turned, careful so as to not awaken her. And he had never fallen asleep.

He'd made it through the next day, and into the night. Although he'd felt tired at eight, he had not gone to bed till midnight, and by then his second wind had arrived, or maybe his third or even fourth. Sleep had been far away, and had never come closer. So tonight he went to bed near nine, when he felt that first flush of drowsiness, the settling of his body for the night. Now it's later. He doesn't know how much later because he's already turned his clock to the wall.

Downstairs, he hears the sound of the television: Barbara's undoubtedly watching a movie. Closer, the clock in the hall. Closer still, his own breathing, to which he tries to pay attention. Breathe in, then out. In, then out. Still no sleep.

He's not tired, and he's not frustrated. He's just still, as memories float toward the surface of his consciousness. If they interest him, he follows them.

He remembers last fall, a couple of days after he made love with Barbara. In this memory, it's still dark, though getting brighter. A man and boy walk slowly through a forest. He is the man and the boy is his son. He sees the scene as he sees so many of his memories, and as he sees so much of his life, from an outside perspective, from some sort of objective vantage point. Like a movie. In this movie, Gordon is in front. They hold guns.

It's that time of morning when trees, bushes, and even grasses began to materialize before your eyes. The shapes remain blurred by a fog that clings tightly to the ground and reduces the world to the space from this bush to that tree, from the stump behind them becoming vague before fading out entirely to the jumble of boulders now taking form ahead.

When they first got out of the pickup an hour earlier, it was dark enough that Gordon was forced to load the carbines by touch—eight rounds into his own gun, and two into his son Stewart's: if Stewart was going to hump his gun all day through the woods, as he had the day before, the extra weight of every cartridge counted. Larry is proud that his son, though only eleven, has never complained. Sometimes Larry worries about the toughness of his son. But not so far this trip.

They stop and listen. Gordon hears nothing but his own shallow breathing and the slight scraping of small rocks as he shifts his weight. The fog collapses the world of sounds, too, until nothing exists outside their immediate surroundings.

The day before had been the first time he'd brought Stewart hunting. It hadn't been the first time they'd tramped these mazes of hills and gulleys together—the entire family walked here often during the summer—but it was the first time they'd brought guns. Gordon had been looking forward to this trip since long before Stewart was born.

The land has belonged to the family for a couple hundred years now, since his ancestor Miles Gordon settled and cleared it, first of Indians, then of forests. The seven generations of Gordons since had been born here, raised families here, died here. Most were buried here. This is where he belongs.

He remembers a day spent here with his own father. Larry must have been nine. His father took him for a walk atop a rocky ridge. It was crisp. The leaves were turning. He was in love with his father's long strides that never waited for him to catch up. They hiked all through the afternoon, and at last stopped at the edge of a steep slope. Larry could tell his father was going to say something important. For one awful moment he thought his father would throw his arms wide and say, "Someday, my son, all this will be yours." While that would have been true, Larry thanked the Lord his father didn't just come out and say it. But Gordon never forgot what his father did say: "There is something that separates you from all others, like this ridge separates two valleys. That difference brings with it responsibilities. Don't ever forget that you're a Gordon, and that Gordons have made this country what it is."

Standing there, in the fog, he tells that story to his son. He can't point to a geological divide to make his point, but he believes Stewart understands it nonetheless.

Man and boy now breathe heavily. It has been a strenuous morning. They've already walked a couple of miles in the slow pace of the hunter: step, pause, listen, step. Gordon leans toward his son, then points to the trunk of a tree. "A rub," he says. "A buck has been marking his territory, rubbing the velvet off his antlers."

Stewart nods.

Now Gordon points up a grassy slope to where a boulder, framed by two large pine trees, provides cover. "We go up there."

They climb the slope, then crouch behind the rock, leaning against it and cradling their weapons. Soon they see a chipmunk, then sparrows. Quail, and eventually a cock pheasant. They wait. Gordon's muscles grow tight, and his joints began to stiffen. Stewart begins to shiver. The fog never lifts. Gordon is proud of his son for sitting still. He'd come hunting with a nephew once, and for three hours the child didn't stop humming and playing imaginary drums. For three hours they hadn't seen a living creature.

Gordon and Stewart wait. And then they see it, through the fog. A slender shape, a darker gray coalescing out of the mist, lightening in color to tan, the edges sharpening till they see a deer. Gordon whispers, "Probably a doe. The big boy sent her out to make sure it's safe." The doe—Gordon's right—cautiously makes her way up the draw. A step. A step. Nose up. A white-tail. She looks their direction, but neither freezes nor bolts. She begins to trot. They'd not been seen, smelled, or heard.

They wait. When he was younger, Gordon would have given the buck ten or fifteen minutes to show up. Now he knows better. They wait a half-hour, then forty-five minutes. In the far distance they hear the blast of a hunting rifle, the only sound that has made it through the fog. The fog deepens.

Another deer materializes. A big one. It moves slowly up the draw. Is it a male? Gordon whispers, "If you see bone on the head, shoot."

Stewart slips his carbine over the rock, aims. The deer comes closer. Gordon's senses become acute. He hears and smells and sees everything. He sees bone. He says, softly, "Squeeze, just like I taught you."

Nothing.

"Do it."

Still nothing. Gordon looks at his son, and from the side sees him squinting down the barrel. He sees his son's finger tight on the trigger. He says, "Shoot him." Nothing happens.

Gordon shifts, and slowly brings his own rifle over the rock. The buck moves cautiously. There's still time: if the old boy bolts he'll live. Gordon aims for the upper neck so that if he misses he won't wound the animal—his father taught him early that there's no worse sin than to gutshoot a deer—and he fires. The buck falls. Gordon pumps out the spent cartridge and pumps in a live one. He picks up the shell and drops it in his pocket.

Below, the buck struggles to stand, then falls back to the grass. Gordon looks at Stewart, who is ashen. "Come on, son," Gordon says, and begins down the slope.

The buck looks at them. He no longer struggles, but watches almost disinterestedly. He seems to know and accept what's to come next. Gordon stops at about twenty paces, raises his rifle, aims for the forehead, and fires. The buck collapses, like a marionette whose strings have all been cut.

Gordon ejects the cartridge and pops in a fresh one. He says, "Our first kill. What do you think?" He looks at his son, whose face still reveals no emotion, still holds no blood.

Gordon bends to pick up the shell, and his son walks past him. The boy approaches the buck, then leans to touch the soft muzzle with his fingers. His father rushes up to step hard on the animal's neck. "Watch it, Stew! If he's alive he'll kill you."

The child stands, and now at last Gordon sees that his son is crying. He pauses a moment, then turns to his son and holds him close round the shoulders.

His son only stares quietly into the fog.

Malia and Dennis sit in the back booth at Chan's Dragon Inn, a few blocks from the Council. Malia pokes at her food. She'd gotten, as usual, General Tso's chicken, and as usual it's overdone and dry. She keeps ordering it because she knows everything else on the menu is worse. She sips her tea, which is surprisingly good. Dennis uses his fork to organize his dried black peppers into a pile, then to mix them in among his meat and vegetables, then to sort them out again.

Cigarette smoke drifts in from Chan's Dragon Lounge— separated from the restaurant by an open doorway filled with hanging beads. Someone in the lounge sings karaoke to *Proud Mary*. His voice, like the food, is just barely passable.

It's late for a work night. Sometime near eleven. They left the office only a half hour ago.

Dennis asks, "Have you had a chance to look at the Vexcorp file?"

"No," she answers. "It's still on my desk. Do you need it?"

"Not yet. I haven't heard again from *60 Minutes*. I'll let you know."

Dennis mixes the peppers back in. The singer completes the song, and a couple of people clap. Dennis asks, "Did you finish that appeal last week?"

Malia nods. "Thank god the post office by the airport stays open so late. Otherwise I'd never have made the cut-off."

Silence.

She continues, "So a lot of my arguments weren't very good."

More silence. A woman in the lounge begins a wretched rendition of *Freebird*. Malia says, "It's all bullshit anyway. The deciding officer at Department of Ecology is the same goon who rubberstamps Vexcorp's permits. He's not gonna overturn his own decision. I'll appeal his rejection. His supervisor will reject my appeal. I'll appeal that rejection, and *his* supervisor will reject *that* appeal. It's a game we play to make ourselves feel useful."

"What about that good inspector?"

"Osborn? Transferred."

"Where?"

"Somewhere he can't do any harm. Maybe forced retirement."

Dennis asks, "Do you think we should sue?"

"About the inspector?"

"No, the expansion—"

"You know we don't have the money. Besides, Vexcorp would just sign on as an intervenor and bury us under mounds of paper. In any case I don't think we can get past Cash's sufficiency language."

"What, then?"

She shrugs. The peppers get sorted. Suddenly both take in a breath to say something.

Malia: "—Do—"

Dennis: "—You—"

Malia: "I'm sorry. Go ahead."

"No, you."

More silence, then Dennis says, "I was just going to say you look beautiful tonight."

"Thank you."

Silence between them.

Dennis asks, "What's wrong?"

Malia shakes her head.

Dennis asks, "What were you going to say?"

A long pause, and finally, "What keeps you going?"

Dennis is caught off guard. "What?"

"In the face of all this shit . . ."

More silence. In the other room the woman, thankfully, begins to wind down. Malia continues, "We've been working together what, five years now, six? I still don't know what motivates you, why you do this work. Even through our relationship I could never get a handle . . ."

"It's the right thing," he says. "I mean the work . . . The relationship, too, of course, but the work . . ."

She nods.

"I feel a certain peace I haven't felt in other work. I never felt this in private practice. I always felt restless, like whatever I did I should be doing something else."

She smiles.

He says again, "It's the right thing."

"What is, exactly?"

"Saving the kids, the river."

"And you'd do anything to save them?"

"Anything legal." He pauses. "And not too dangerous, sure."

"What does that mean?"

Silence. Silence from the other room as well. He asks, "What do you have in mind?"

She shakes her head.

Neither speaks for a while. Malia sips her tea. She smells cigarettes from the lounge and grease from the kitchen. Dennis mixes his peppers again. She asks, "Do you ever despair?"

He looks at her, hard.

She says, "Because the kids keep dying."

"You know that doesn't work. Emotions are luxuries I can't afford. *We* can't afford. Not about work. If I would have called *60 Minutes* all pissed off about dead kids they'd have dismissed me as just another loser who hates the system. I can't get that label. I always think of a description I read seven or eight years ago in the newspaper. Before I became an activist. They were calling some environmentalist 'a Chicken Little extremist who runs around making unfounded assaults on industry.' That really stuck with me. I can't get that label. I don't want to lose credibility."

"With whom?"

"I don't understand."

"Credibility with whom? The kids or the newspaper?"

Dennis doesn't say anything.

Malia says, "That was me they were describing."

"Oh," he says, looking at his plate.

She doesn't say anything.

He clears his throat, says, "Interesting."

She is still silent.

He says, "Maybe that's why your appeals always get turned down. You don't speak their language. You don't play their game."

"I've been playing their game for years. Since long before you joined the Council."

More silence. Finally Dennis says, evenly, "It sounds like you need a vacation."

Malia looks away, to the front of the restaurant. A young black woman walks in, waits for someone to seat her. She's wearing the shortest dress Malia has ever seen. It's black, and comes down in the front and back to at most an inch below her crotch. It flares on the sides to reveal the hollows in her buttocks. Malia wonders how she sits, or walks, for that matter.

Malia looks back at Dennis. She says, slowly, "Sometimes I feel the only things that keep me going are rage and sorrow . . ."

"You definitely need a vacation."

"Something's gotta break. Who was it who defined insanity as doing the same thing over and over and expecting different results?"

"I don't know," he says dismissively.

"I can't keep playing this game much longer."

He starts. "Malia. You can't quit—"

"—I—"

"—It's just burnout—"

"—I'm not gonna quit—"

"—Remember—"

"—I need to change the rules—"

"—Remember that Edward Abbey quote about how important it is to be a half-hearted fanatic?"

She says, "I've always hated that quote."

"That's why you're burned out."

"I'm not burned out. I'm breaking down—"

"—Oh, my god. Get some outside interests. Take a rest—"

"—there's a difference."

"Breaking down? Shit, woman."

"It's terrible, but it's a good thing, too. I can't play the game a new way until I've given up on the old. And I hate this fucking language. 'Playing the game.' A fucking game. I can't see the kids as pawns, and I can't see them as statistics."

"But breaking down . . ."

"What's wrong with giving up control?"

Dennis looks honestly alarmed. "Are you going to start frothing at the mouth? Sobbing hysterically?"

Her gaze flashes from Dennis's face to the young woman.

The server, an ancient Chinese woman with white hair pulled into a tight bun, leads the young woman to a table. She sits alone.

Dennis says, "I didn't think you were this jaded."

"I'm not jaded. I'm sick of it."

Dennis shakes his head. "This is the burnout talking. Stress. God, you don't just need a vacation, you need to get la—" He stops, says, "You need, ah, a massage or something."

"What?"

"Something to relax you."

Her jaws go tight. She says, quiet yet sharp: "I don't need to fucking relax. None of us need to fucking relax. Kids are dying. Rivers are dying. The whole fucking planet is dying, and I need to get laid? Give me a fucking break."

"I just thought . . ."

Silence. She wonders, when things go wrong for the young woman in the short skirt, do men, too, think she needs to get laid? Maybe the woman has internalized this message until that's what she thinks, too.

Dennis asks, "You gonna work anymore tonight?"

She stands. "I thought you said I needed a break, needed a massage."

He reaches for her hand, and says, "I'm sorry."

She pulls her hand away.

He says, "You gonna go home?"

She nods.

"Will you be okay walking to the bus?"

She nods again.

"Sure you wouldn't like a ride?"

Dennis is trying. She could meet him halfway. "No thanks. It'd be out of your way."

"I wouldn't mind."

She shakes her head.

"Or you could just come over. Spend the night."

She doesn't say anything, instead trying to process what he said. Finally she understands. She says, "Dennis." Then she shakes her head, says, "I need to go home."

He says a little too quickly, "I didn't mean it that way. I meant you could stay on the couch."

She smiles weakly to grant him the face-saving lie. "Thanks. I'll take the bus."

"Okay," he says.

The server brings the ticket and they pay for their meals. As they walk from the restaurant, Malia looks out of the corners of her eyes at Dennis, watches him stare at the young woman. The young woman smiles at him. Beyond the smile Malia sees something else, a strange distance manifested in the tautness of her muscles. Malia suddenly notices how closely a smile can resemble a grimace. She thinks of bared teeth, of threats and the warding off of threats. If cornered, Malia wonders, would this woman bite back, or would she submit? Perhaps she believes it's only through submission that she can survive at all. Malia wonders what it would take for the woman to bite back. She wonders that for herself, and for Dennis as well.

Dennis walks Malia to the office, to where his car is parked in the lot.

"I'll see you tomorrow?" he asks.

"Yeah. Tomorrow."

He backs out, and pulls away. She watches his taillights disappear around the corner.

Dear Anthony,

Until I got mugged, I had only one other experience with physical violence. Oh sure, there's the violence of the system, of schooling, of the wage economy, of poisons and cancers, of cops protecting the rich, of living on a planet being murdered, and in an entirely different context of course I experienced violence by growing up on a farm and being responsible for the deaths of the plants and animals I ate. But only once had I experienced this sort of fist-in-your-face violence.

It was in a relationship I began perhaps a year after you and I broke up. The man's name was Matt. It was a terrible relationship, even less deserving of the name than I guess what passes for so many relationships.

I've often thought that particular relationship was like the job my mom insisted I take during high school. I don't remember if I ever told you about this. My sophomore year my mom drove me to all the local fast food restaurants, then waited in the car while I filled out applications. I got a job at a place called Round the Corner Hamburgers, an upscale burger joint with a phone at each booth for ordering, and, if I remember right, twenty-nine types of hamburgers. I hated the job and everything about it: its meaninglessness and tedium, its absurdity. Most of all I hated the way the acceptance of drudgery insinuated itself through this job into my life. When after three months I finally told my mom I couldn't stand it any longer and was going to quit, with or without her approval, she said, "You lasted a lot longer than I expected. I only wanted you to do it so you'd know for the rest of your life what you don't want to do."

I guess the one good thing about my time with Matt was that I recognized traits I don't want in my life. I hated his aggression and his need to control. He was rich, which repulsed me. Or more precisely, I was repulsed by his attitude toward wealth. He was fascinated by money, what it could buy, what it enabled him to do, and especially the subtle and sometimes not-so-subtle ways it affected the balance of power in all of his relationships, including his with me.

Most crucially, Matt was violent. Not physically, until the end, but emotionally. He picked fights over nothing, and he always had to win. He was insecure, jealous. He despised my family, and let me know it.

You could easily ask, why was I with him? I asked myself that, too, even then. All I can say is that we all make mistakes. We all sometimes only see what we want to see and blind ourselves to everything else.

I ended the relationship one evening in late June. I'd brought him up to my parents'. Something snapped inside, and in the middle

of yet another argument (about you, actually) I suddenly began to put
his clothes into his duffel bag. He shouted for me to stop. My parents
weren't at home. He balled his fists and stalked toward me. I stopped
what I was doing, and said to him, "You can hit me, but you can't
make me stay in this relationship. I'm through."

I think what snapped inside was that just as the job had insinuated the acceptance of drudgery into my life, so Matt was insinuat-
ing the acceptance of emotional violence. If we see it around us, if daily
we bathe and swim in it, how can it not seep into our pores?

The wonderful thing is that as I said I was through with him,
I felt a rush of energy, as if through all my time with him I had been
fighting not only him but myself. No longer having to force down my
own feelings, and no longer bound to him, I felt more fully alive than
anytime I could remember in that relationship.

He continued to shout, but I didn't respond. When I finished
packing, I said, "You can either come with me to the car, or you can
wait till my parents come back and my father will take you. But by
then the bus will be gone and you'll probably have to spend the night at
the station. Your call."

It would be nice to say my resolve convinced him to do the
right thing, but that wouldn't be true. The truth is that he called me
names I will never repeat, and then he beat me. I tried to talk sense
into him, and he beat me worse. I tried to call 911, and he pulled
the phone from the wall. I understood in that moment that because
his violence made no sense to me—I'm presuming it did to him, since
otherwise he wouldn't have done it—to try to rationally talk him out
of it was to invite further abuse. It was, in fact, to fall into his mad-
ness. There were only two realistic responses: one was to get away, and
the other was to kill him. I chose the former. I escaped, ran to the barn,
and hid in one of the equipment rooms. He looked for me, and tried to
apologize and call me out, but gave up after a while. Realizing that my
father—and also my mother—would probably have killed him when
they got back, he left a note saying he was sick of my attitude, that I
was making a big mistake, and that finally I had pushed him too far.
He used my car to drive himself to the station (and keyed it before

leaving). The bus was gone by the time my parents got home. I talked them out of filing charges: I just wanted him out of my life.

I thought a lot about that relationship in the years after, and especially these past couple of years that I've been on the run, and I've long since come to the conclusion that had I not been able to get to the barn—had there been no way for me to get away—and especially had I been forced to stay in this relationship over time, one of us would have ended up dead. Maybe not that night, but eventually. In all the years since that relationship, I've been able to come up with no compelling reason that it should have been me.

Dennis drives the streets alone, listless, like a burro following his daily path from pasture to barn. Left. Right. Another right. He barely notices when a stoplight turns red, and pays no mind as he brakes the car to a stop. Just as automatically he accelerates when the light turns green.

It never feels like night on this thoroughfare, with streetlamps casting double and triple shadows that rotate around him as he drives. He rolls down his window to listen to the sound of the engine echoing off the tall buildings to the side.

He thinks of Malia, of the dinner, of the conversation. He hates to admit it, but he's still in love with her. He doesn't think the relationship meant much to her, but it remains his most unforgettable and intense. At first he had liked the intensity. But he had soon realized he liked the intensity better from a distance: as their brief romantic relationship was ending, he complained to a friend, "I like a little fire in the fireplace now and then, but that woman would burn down the fucking house."

He starts up the on-ramp to the interstate. It's a short and steep climb from street level to the long concrete bridge that carries traffic from one end of the city to the other while insulating it from the city itself. The ramp challenges his old Civic, and he keeps the gas pedal to the floor. Once on the bridge, at the beast's max cruising speed of fifty-five, he pulls in behind a UPS semi. The interstate is busy. Like the streetlamps, it never sleeps.

He can't get Malia out of his mind. He's upset at himself for propositioning her. How had he expected her to respond?

But what was he supposed to do? Was he supposed to stifle his own feelings? It's what he feels, dammit: he still wants her. Some evenings working alone late at the Council he wanders into her office just to sit in her chair, to look at notes she's left to herself for the next day, notes in her sharp, sloping handwriting. Every once in a while he gets the urge to write something and leave it for her to find, but of course he never does: he's in love; he's not a stalker.

It's late. He's tired. He feels empty as the streets below. He wants someone to have sex with. Not just sex, which he knows would ultimately make him feel even emptier, but something more. He wants someone to reach him, to touch him. He wants to feel. Right now, right here. He wants Malia, and if he can't have *her*, he wants somebody. He wants somebody to want him. He doesn't so much want intercourse, though he would never turn that down, as he wants to lightly kiss a woman, and feel her body arch toward him. He wants to watch her kiss his fingertips, and to know that's what she wants.

He thinks about the woman in the restaurant, with her short dress and her long, slender arms. Her skin so dark. He's never been with a black woman. What would that be like? Different? He doesn't think so. It's like that guy said in the Bible about vanity: everything is nothing.

Dennis is in the slow lane. A car passes on his left. He glances over. It's a woman in her late forties. She smiles. She looks good to him. Even in the relative dark of her car, he can make out traces of gray in her dark hair, and that makes her look even better. He likes gray hair. Maturity. Wisdom. Those are good things. He smiles back. She drives on.

A moment, he thinks. A moment's connection—even through layers of glass, and even rolling at eighty feet per second on rubber tires across a concrete ribbon—still means something.

He has to laugh. It's all so absurd. Have our relationships become so frail that such a contact as this is enough to lift us? And these teases, these artificial contacts, are everywhere. What's the difference between the smile from the woman at the restaurant and the smiles of the women who beckon to him every night from his television, from advertisements, promising an end to loneliness, promising fantastic sex, promising the possibility of burying himself in their flesh and in their hearts if only he will buy their product? At least the woman on the highway isn't selling anything.

We have, he thinks, forgotten what is real. We follow ribbons of concrete from the hollow shells of our offices to the hollow shells of our apartments, and never have a human interaction with another human being. We drift from fuck to fuck and job to job, and what the hell does any of it mean? What's real?

Last week a woman called the office. She thought that since they were the Council Against Toxics, they might be able to help her boy. She thought her child might have ingested poison, and she thought they were doctors. Janet Herman, her name was. Her son Joey was vomiting blood. Dennis told her to call the hospital. She said he might die. "Call 911," he said.

"Can't you do something?"

No, he remembers thinking, *we can't do a damn thing*.

It's all such a fucking mess.

God, he wants a woman. Someone to hold him, to say to him, "Dennis, shhh, it's okay." No one ever says that to him. No one ever picks up *his* pieces when he falls apart. And so he doesn't fall apart. He just drives the concrete ribbon to and from the office, he watches a little TV, he tries to meet women when he can, and tries to keep thinking that the kids are nothing more than statistics. Even goddamn Joey Herman vomiting his guts out. Nothing more than a goddamn statistic, probably just another kid who's gonna die of cancer of the stomach.

⊕

Larry Gordon still can't sleep. He lies in bed, unmoving. Memories rise and fall like waves. Some of these he hasn't considered in years. He remembers the man who introduced him to Barbara: a mutual friend they both soon—for reasons they couldn't name—grew to detest. He pictured the man's face, and tried unsuccessfully to uncover where he had first met him. That image passes, and he thinks about rare trips in the company limo to the downtown Vexcorp factory. He remembers looking through mirrored and bulletproof glass to the faces of those on the outside, and remembers feeling glad he'd been born who he was.

He takes a deep breath, then lets it out slowly. The next image is of a private secretary he'd had to fire probably a half-dozen years ago. Her name was June. June Karr. She was good. Too bad he'd had to let her go.

He remembers the morning of her firing. The door to his office in the uptown headquarters opens, and June—already now no longer his secretary, though she doesn't yet know it for certain—walks in. She stares at him, holds out a piece of paper. She asks, "What's this?"

Gordon sets down the sandwich he's been eating, brushes the crumbs onto his napkin. Though his memory is not normally this precise, to this day he remembers the scatter pattern of the crumbs on the white cloth. He says, "Your freedom."

Silence between them.

She says, "Twenty years, and this is what—"

"—You thought—"

"—I'm not some assembly-line worker you can lay off—"

"—you'd won, didn't you?"

She shakes her head weakly. "Won?"

All these years later he still isn't sure if she'd been faking her confusion.

He stares at the sandwich. Reuben. The room smells of corned beef and sauerkraut. He says, "Yes, won. But it takes more than that—"

"—Winning? I'm talking about supporting my family."

"Yes," he says. "You *were* family." More silence, before he says abruptly, "Where did you turn when your husband left?"

"What does that have to do with—"

"—Now you're the one . . ." He trails off.

"I have no idea what you're talking about."

"Don't lie to me," he says.

She looks away.

He begins again, "To reveal private information . . ." Another pause. *Finally*, "You don't understand how people are. They're stupid. They're sheep. They're children. They need to be told the facts of life . . . They don't need to be scared."

"You think I leaked the notes."

"It's not my job to think. It's my job to know. That's why I win. Always. You're lucky you're only losing your job."

More confused than angry: "Are you threatening me?"

"I'm just telling you how things are. You betrayed me, and you betrayed the company. It took a lot of work to control the damage. We're fortunate Chris at the newspaper is a reasonable man and called us before printing something stupid." He'd looks at the sandwich, then back up to her. He says, "Now get out of here. I don't ever want to see you again."

"Twenty years . . ."

"And this is what you do. Pathetic."

Tears start to fall. "I need the job."

He says, softly, "Don't grovel. It's humiliating."

She says, "I won't . . ."

He brings his sandwich halfway to his mouth, then returns it to the desk. He says, "Do it again? You should have thought of that before you leaked the notes."

"My kids."

"Not my problem. My problem is running this company. You should have considered your children before you decided to become a social reformer."

"Twenty years."

"You said that."

She leaves. He looks at his watch. Five minutes. He's glad it went quickly. He hadn't wanted a scene. Embarrassing. Unnecessary. Now it's done. He picks up his sandwich, stares for a moment at a loose strand of cabbage, and takes another bite.

He'd never seen her again.

It's late. Malia's tired. Despite what she said earlier to Dennis, she's a little nervous. She's alone on the street. In the distance she hears the hum of traffic on the interstate—which she tries unsuccessfully to convince herself is the sound of the river—and the hard soles of her shoes clack loudly on the sidewalk.

She walks past darkened stores, and past a small abandoned hotel. An empty parking garage. A car drives by, then another. And then she is alone again.

When Malia was a child she sometimes pretended that whatever she saw was the view through the lens for a camera filming a horror movie. Her gaze—the camera—would linger on an open doorway, the stairs to the cellar, the shadows in back beneath the lilac bushes, and the lingering itself would lend significance to the glance; why would the camera linger on shadows unless the shadows held something to fear? Then she would run to the room where her father sat reading, or to her own room, where she would leap into bed, then turn on her lamp and read a nice book, a happy book, until she was no longer scared. Now, as an adult, Malia forgets about that game for months or even years, then suddenly remembers it on nights like this.

Remembering the game gives momentum to her fear, as though she had been swimming against its current, then suddenly turned to go with the flow. This is not a good neighborhood in which to walk alone. At night and often in the day most visitors drive with their doors locked, praying for no car trouble. Many run stop signs at night so they'll never be stationary targets. Anything to avoid being caught here. But here she is, as she is so many nights. Only tonight she's even later than usual.

She makes it to the arterial. Just one more block. Now the clacking of her shoes is more reassuring than frightening, no longer a measure of vulnerability. She begins to feel sheepish for her fear, and to wonder if her concern is racist and classist—many of the people in this neighborhood are black or Hispanic, and nearly all are poor. Would she feel this same fear walking the country roads near her parents' farm? She wouldn't be so concerned even near her own apartment, in a neighborhood not quite so poor as this.

She makes it to the bus stop. It's well-lit. Glass encloses the three sides away from the street. The bus should be here soon.

A man approaches. He's young, maybe twenty-four, with brown skin and cornrows. He's about five-eight with a muscular build. He's wearing a white shirt, Girbaud jeans, and a pair of Timberland boots. His smile reveals a flash of gold. She hopes he'll continue walking.

He doesn't. Instead he stops at the kiosk. After looking at the bus schedule, he steps close to her. Both look straight ahead, toward the street. Malia feels the pressure of his arm against hers, and she shifts slightly away. He moves close again, and again she shifts.

He asks, "Is there a problem?"

She hesitates, then says, "I like a little space." A pause, then, "I've been working inside all day."

He considers her, says, "Seems like you got a problem wit me."

The smell of marijuana is overpowering.

She says, "I'm just waiting for the bus."

He smiles broadly. She thinks again of a smile's resemblance to a grimace. He says, "Me, too. I never seen you."

"I've never seen you either."

"That's odd," he says, "because I come here all the time wit my friends."

Two more men suddenly appear in the kiosk. One is black, tall, maybe six feet, skinny. He has a low haircut with waves. He's wearing a black and red Mark Ecko sweatsuit and a pair of Nike Air Force Ones, black with red soles. The other is white, short, kind of scrawny, with long greasy dark hair. His hollow eyes look like they're staring at her, but she realizes quickly they're not looking at anything. He smiles, showing brown and yellow teeth inside dry lips. He stinks, of body odor, liquor, and, slightly, urine. His clothes, a hooded sweatshirt and corduroys, are too big for him. She notices his fingers are burnt and discolored. She's worked here long enough to know this is the mark of a long time crack user. She realizes she's in serious trouble.

She says, "Shit. What do you want?"

The first man looks at her. "Just waitin for the bus."

No one says anything. The other two look at Malia appreciatively. The first man stares openly. Finally he says, "Looks like you could use some fun."

She ignores him.

He continues, "Wanna come kick it wit us?"

She says, "No, thank you. I need to go home."

The man asks, "What? You got a problem? First you move away, and now you don't want to party wit us?"

"I just got off work."

"Workin late? Where's a nice-lookin bitch like you work?"

She turns to face him directly. "I try to protect kids from cancer."

He nods. A moment's silence before he asks, "Do I look sick? You gonna take care of me?"

"Maybe if you're sick," she says, "you should see a doctor."

He says, "No, really, I'm sick. Why don't you examine me?"

Where's the damn bus? "Look," she says. "I don't want any trouble. I just want to go home."

He moves up close again, says quietly, "Listen, you don't got nothin to do."

She backs away, against the glass. "Leave me alone."

"We don't want to leave you alone."

She looks at him closely, then shakes her head. She's too tired for this. She says, "This is bullshit. Do you know why I'm here? Do you?"

"Yeah," the man says, "You're here to party wit us. That's what you want."

She's had it. Something snaps. She says, "Give me a fucking break. I spend all day dealing with corporate assholes who're killing the kids around here, who're killing the river, and this is what you do? If you want my wallet, just take it. But don't give me any fucking bullshit."

The man's eyes open wide in mock surprise. He says, "That's bad language for such a pretty mouth."

"You want my wallet, or not? Or do you just get your kicks by threatening women?"

Finally the other black man, the tall one, speaks. His face is all angles and corners. He says, "Give me yo backpack."

She takes it off her shoulder and hands it to him. She says, "Leave me my bus pass so I can get home."

The second man, with the angles, looks to the first. The first says, "Sure. We don't need no damn bus pass anyway."

The second man rummages through her bag, then hands it to the third. The third man is smug. A vacant smile stays on his face as he looks into the pack and pulls out her wallet. He opens the billfold, ostentatiously pulls out the bus pass, holds it toward her between thumb and forefinger, then lets it fall to the ground. He slips the wallet into his pocket and drops the bag.

The second man says, "Now gimme yo shoes."

She stares at him, uncomprehending, and says, "You have my wallet."

Now he smiles. "Oh, you call the shots? This is *yo* bus corner?"

She thinks, *Where is the bus?*

He continues, "Uh-huh." He pauses before he says, slowly, "Do as you told or I'm gonna mess up yo face."

She kicks off her shoes, then stoops to pick them up. She hands them to the man with the angular face. He hands them to the smirker. The first man stands watching, hand on his chin.

The second man says, "Now the socks."

She says, "Fuck you. You have what you want, now go."

The first one punches her. The back of her head slams against the glass, then she falls forward and to the side. For a moment she doesn't know where she is. Then she remembers. She's sitting on concrete, on a sidewalk. Men. Yes. The first man says, quietly, "You got no idea what we want. Now give me the fuckin socks. I'm not going to tell you again."

She removes her socks, hands them over. He passes them to the third man, who turns them inside out. He reaches also into her shoes. Finally he speaks: "Nothing."

The second man says, "Bitch too fuckin stupid to hide her money. Looks like we'll be seeing you again tomorrow night." He smiles. "And the night after." He leans down, "You sure you don't want to party wit us?"

Her face hurts, as does the back of her head where she hit the glass. She's still confused, doesn't know where she is. And then she begins to understand. She's waiting for the bus. Coming home from work. She has to tear apart another EIS tomorrow. It's late. The Vexcorp refinery is going to expand. But these men. Who are they? She shakes her head and suddenly understands deeper than before, deeper even than with Matt. She stands, says, "Have you heard of Vexcorp?"

The first man looks at her as though she'd asked him if he'd heard of concrete, brick, or razor wire; some inescapable fact of city life. He says, "Yeah?"

Very calm now, she says, "You know what I just realized? There's no difference between corporate assholes and street thugs." She stares at him, asks, "Did you know that?"

"What?" the second man says.

Malia looks at the first man. Not so much angry as focused, she says to him, "You beat up a woman, and that's gonna solve your problems? You're so much like Vexcorp, they probably don't even have to send cops down to keep you in line."

The men seem simultaneously annoyed and amused. The first man, more disturbed by her attitude than the others, responds,

"What the fuck you talkin about?"

She continues, "Are you so stupid you can't make the connection? I already told you I work with kids and cancer."

"What's cancer got to do with—"

She interrupts, "Are you from Mars? What part of cancer don't you understand?"

The man steps up close, his face an inch from hers. "I know more about cancer than you ever will. I seen more people die than . . ."

She cuts him off again. "Why do you think I'm here? People are dying. The river is fucked. That's why I'm here. And you, you're big enough to beat me up. What are you gonna do, take my money and stop the cancer?"

He pushes her against the glass wall, says "Fuck you, bitch. Just fuck you."

In an instant, the second man has a knife in his hand. He begins to move close.

The first man waves him away, says, "She's mine."

Malia feels no emotion. No fear. No hope. No hopelessness. She is just alert. She sees details clearly: the dark patch under the man's jaw where he missed shaving, the texture of his shirt, the slight movement of his chest as he inhales. Smells become distinct, and precise. There is the marijuana, his sweat, his own slight fear. She smells the street, and the stale smell of the city. She feels her blood push through the veins of her arms. She hears the blood in her ears. She doesn't struggle in his grip. He looks at her closely, then turns his head slightly at an angle, almost as though he were going to kiss her. He pushes her harder against the glass, and she thinks, *He could kill me right now*. He begins to shake slightly, not so she can see it, only enough that she can feel it. His lips purse tight as though he's holding back years of words or spittle or anger. He gets tears in his eyes.

Now she's scared. This could be it. She realizes he actually could kill her, and that somewhere far beyond a conscious level that decision—whether to kill her or let her live—is being made. No one speaks.

Finally the second man gently touches his shoulder.

The first man says, as much to himself as to anyone else, "We're out of here." He turns away from Malia, and the other two follow. Malia slides down the glass. The second man looks back at her, stares hard. He glances at the backs of his friends, then toward Malia, and in one quick motion lifts the pack and tosses it softly toward her. He joins the others.

Once the men are safely around a corner, Malia begins to sob.

Ray-Ray starts to say something, then stops. He starts again, "Why—"

Dujuan cuts him off, "Don't fuckin ask."

"You don't even know what—"

"—Don't fuckin go there. It don't matter."

"Okay," Ray-Ray says, then under his breath, "Dumb-ass nigga."

Dujuan says, "I can't hear you. Don't talk under yo breath."

"I didn't even say nothin."

Dujuan barks, "That's what I thought."

Silence.

Dujuan says, "You ain't the only one who . . ."

Ray-Ray asks, "Who what?" Though he asks, he knows without asking—but could not possibly have articulated, nor even brought anywhere near consciousness—the rest of Dujuan's sentence: *You're not the only one with a hundred emotions scratching at your guts, trying to get out. You're not the only one who sometimes needs to hit someone to prove you're alive.*

Dujuan says, "Nothin. Just forget about it."

There's a silence before Ray-Ray says, "Forgotten."

There's another silence before Simon says, from the back seat, "Why don't you hit the radio?"

Ray-Ray turns it on, but doesn't pay attention. He's

thinking about those emotions scratching to get out, and he's thinking about violence. He doesn't consider himself a violent man, even though he has hurt a lot of people. He's beaten them, cut them, put a cap in their ass: whatever Dujuan wants him to do or what he feels like doing himself because somebody isn't giving him what he wants. But in his own mind he isn't violent, because he's never killed anyone.

Or so he says.

But that isn't true. He *has* killed someone. Two people, in fact, although the second one doesn't count.

He killed his first human on a sunny, windy day in April a couple of years ago. It was one of those spring days when sunshine makes all the difference in the world. Step into it and you're warm in short sleeves. Step into a shadow and you're chilled in a coat. He'd been in the sun, so it felt like June. He was kicking it downtown, nothing to do, wandering window to window looking not so much inside the pawn shops, record stores, and sorry diners—he couldn't have seen the interiors anyway because of the glare—as at the spears of sunlight reflecting off the glass. They'd hurt and dazzled him, and he'd liked it.

Ray-Ray'd caught himself thinking that, and almost laughed. Staring at reflected sunlight? He was boring himself silly.

He'd turned a corner and passed from sun to shade, also leaving the lee of a building. The wind caught him in the face. It was no longer June, but February. A few steps, and he ducked into an alley. He followed it. Eventually it opened into a sunny, calm alcove. Dumpsters and shuttered back doors of businesses lined crumbling brick walls.

A man slept curled in a bright corner. Ray-Ray walked to him. The man was a bum, with long dirty blonde hair and a beard the color of dead grass. Ray-Ray saw a can of hair spray a few feet away. "Fucking waste," he said.

He stood, nodding for a moment, then quietly slipped his gun out of its resting place beneath his jacket and under his belt in back. He cocked the gun, softly, then leaned way low. He brought the gun as close as he could to the man's forehead without touching it. "Right here," he said. "I got you."

He hadn't wanted to shoot; he'd just wanted to hold this other's life in his hands, for no reason other than he could. No orders from Dujuan. No theft. No nothing. Just pure. He'd wanted to feel the purity of that juice. Twenty seconds. Thirty. It felt good. He laughed silently: this sure beat hell out of staring at reflected spears of sunlight.

Then he noticed something. The man's eyes. They were open. Glazed but open. Ray-Ray felt exposed, like the bum knew what he was thinking. Ray-Ray jumped, not much, but enough to accidentally touch the gun against the man's skin and to accidentally pull the trigger. A flash. A blast. The man's head jerked and its back exploded.

Ray-Ray stared a moment at the hole in the man's forehead, the black of burn, the pink skin pulled back around the edges, the star-shaped lacerations of the contact wound, the white of bone mixed with the black and gray of soot, the gray of brain, the clean red of blood. He started to shake. He didn't so much like this feeling anymore.

He put away his gun, looked quickly around to make sure nobody had seen him, then began to walk, calmly as he could, toward the far opening of the alley. He turned the corner, walked a couple of blocks, and caught the first bus that happened by.

Nothing ever came of the killing. So far as he knew, the police never checked into it. It had just been another drunk guy— brain addled from huffing hair spray and god knows what other shit—found dead, this one with a couple of holes in his skull. But Ray-Ray had seen him die. It was because of Ray-Ray. He would never forget that.

The Christmas wreath still hangs on the door to Dennis's apartment. Every day when he comes home from work he tells himself to take it down, and every day after he goes inside he forgets about it. The same is true tonight.

He flips on the lights, walks straight to the kitchen, opens the refrigerator—even though he just ate—stares inside, finds nothing he wants, and shuts it again. He goes to the living room and sits on the couch, then leafs through an issue of *Audubon* on the coffee table. After he puts down *Audubon* he picks up *Newsweek*. He drops it, too. *Shit*, he thinks, *it's all just shit*.

He moves from the couch to the recliner. He punches the remote, but before noticing what's on television decides he needs a beer. When he returns from the fridge, brown bottle in hand, an advertisement is on the tube. The ad, for a truck, shows some goon four-wheeling it through a stream bed. *Destroying habitat*, he thinks before he can catch himself. Immediately after that he thinks, *Damn that Malia, she's infected me*.

He reaches toward the magazines on the coffee table before deciding they aren't worth the effort. Then he gets comfortable in his chair, shakes his head, looks at the television, and flips to the premium channels. He makes his way to the upper end, scanning slowly for an interesting plot, a bit of action, or failing either of those, a touch of skin. Not seeing anything, he leans back his chair, sips his beer, and long after it's finished, falls asleep to an old black-and-white movie.

Dennis isn't the only person who watches television late that night. Barbara does, too. She watches movies. Several. She does this often. Nearly every night she watches at least one, or frequently two. That doesn't mean she isn't particular. For her birthday each year, her son Stewart gives her a comprehensive guide to movies, and then throughout the year she checks off every movie she sees. Movies she especially likes she records and stores in a closet devoted to her collection. So far she has over two thousand.

To keep the DVDs organized she numbers them and cross-references them in a three-ring notebook. She resents that Gordon often chuckles when he sees the notebook, and even moreso when he sees her record another movie. He says, "You do know, honey, that we can afford to just buy it." But she doesn't want to buy the film: she wants to watch it, record it, and categorize it in her book.

She goes through phases. In the 1980s it was a lengthy Alfred Hitchcock phase, during which she saw nearly all of his seventy-some films, including his early silent ones. Some of them she'd been forced to rent by mail. Then she went through a foreign language phase, during which she was especially taken by the Japanese. At parties she'd often say, with equal parts bewilderment and understated outrage, "With all the expensive trash that gets made these days, can you believe Akira Kurasawa couldn't get funding to make a final film?" Most of her friends had never heard of Akira Kurasawa, which bothered her even more.

After that came something of a return to her youth as she expanded her collection of film noir, which she had liked very much growing up. There was something that attracted her to the crude and direct yet poetic justice in these films. She couldn't have said precisely what it was she liked, but she watched them again and again.

Most recently she's found herself attracted to erotic films, or erotic scenes in other movies. Not pornography, which she finds even more boring than tasteless, but romance, stories in which men and women fall in love and stay that way. She doesn't know how long this phase will last, though, because these films are as unsatisfactory in their own way as pornography. Usually the movie ends in that blush of intense love and attraction, that magical first connection. She always wants to know what happens next, after the two people, madly in love, create a life together. She wants to know how they maintain their passion, how they maintain their love. She wants to know what happens if they begin to grow apart.

Her favorite erotic scene right now involves Julie Christie and Donald Sutherland—from an early 1970s film by Nicholas Roeg—in which the shots of the sex are interspersed with shots of the two of them preparing for dinner or walking out the door of their hotel. Sex is presented as a part of the dailiness of their lives.

She watches that scene again and again, and wonders when and how the dailiness and normality of sex and even love disappeared from her own life. She wonders more and more often when and where she went wrong.

They continue to drive. Ray-Ray still thinks about violence. The man in the alley isn't the only person he has killed. Ray-Ray killed his cousin Ricky, too. But that doesn't count: that killing was more gift than murder, more an expression of familial responsibility than violence.

Ray-Ray thinks back to last summer, in the back bedroom of his Aunt Claire's apartment.

As he does almost every afternoon—and toward the end it becomes several times each day—Ray-Ray enters without knocking, and makes his way down the hall. He passes the living room and notices that today Claire isn't watching television; she sits silently on the couch. For a moment, he considers going in to talk with her, but instead he walks into the kitchen and turns on the tap. He waits till the water is hot, then partially fills a glass. He pulls a spoon from the drawer. The silence in the apartment disturbs him, and he thinks again about asking Claire what's wrong. But he guesses he knows, and if so, it's better, he decides, to just not talk about it. He walks out of the kitchen and to the rear of the apartment. The door to the back bedroom is slightly ajar, as it is each time he comes.

Ray-Ray slips inside. He doesn't turn on the light. While he waits for his eyes to adjust, he listens for the soft sound of breathing that will tell him Ricky made it through another six hours.

Ricky grew up in this apartment, in this room, then left to live on his own, and at thirty-four came home to die. He has cancer, as his father did before him, and also his uncle. Cancer has become something of a tradition in this family, a sorrowful birthright that comes to them by way of where they live.

Ray-Ray hears Ricky say, quietly, "Still here, bro."

Ray-Ray has a hard time hearing the words, and can just barely make out a dark form on the bed.

"Your stuff," Ricky says, before taking another breath, "It don't work . . ."

Ray-Ray doesn't say anything.

Ricky continues, "It hurts."

The ticking of a clock in the hallway. Ricky's breathing, shallow and uneven, and Ray-Ray's own, too loud in the quiet of the room. Finally, Ray-Ray says, "We got to—"

Ricky cuts him off, "No hospitals."

Chemo. Surgery. He's been through it all. Nothing has helped. Nothing except the shit Ray-Ray hooked him on, and which he now gives him several times a day. It was enough of a struggle to get Ricky to go to the hospital in the first place: his father died in one, hands tied to bed railings to keep him from pulling out the feeding tubes.

Ricky says, "Too late."

"No—"

"I talked to Mom . . ."

"No."

"You said . . ."

Silence, until Ray-Ray says, "I know what I said."

More silence. The clock, the breathing, the sound of his blood pounding in his ears. It would be easy for Ray-Ray to walk out right now and never come back, to pretend the pain in the room is nothing to him. It would be easy, too, to try to talk Ricky out of the decision, as Ray-Ray and Claire had talked him out of it before. But the first isn't an option: it's not how family acts. As for the other, it's pure selfishness: to put off Ricky's death for another day or two or three would be doing no favors to Ricky. But Ray-Ray hates to do this. He hates to be the one.

"Cover your eyes," Ray-Ray says, and turns on the light. He looks at Ricky and hates what he sees. Hollow cheeks. Protruding forehead with deep hollows at the temples. Stick-like fingers covering sunken eye sockets. Ray-Ray looks away.

He puts the glass on the nightstand, then reaches into a drawer beneath, which he resupplied only a few days ago. He pulls out the plastic that holds the tar heroin, and unwraps it. He nearly retches at the bitter, vinegary stench, as happens each time he opens the package. He wouldn't do this for someone else. The heroin is dark, and tacky to the touch. He uses a pocket knife to scrape a dose into the spoon. He triples the dose just to be sure.

Between breaths, Ricky asks, "You know how much?"

"Yes," Ray-Ray lies, and triples it again. He considers giving him the whole damn chunk. No need to save it, since Ray-Ray doesn't use, Claire sure as hell doesn't, and there's no way he's going to feed any of Simon's habits.

Neither speaks as Ray-Ray rewraps the chunk, then pours a little hot water into the spoon and stirs it to dissolve the tar. Then Ray-Ray draws the liquid through a piece of cotton as a filter into the syringe. But there's too much junk for the gear. He'll have to slam him a couple of times.

Ricky extends his arm—a useless gesture, since the veins are gone—and Ray-Ray says, "There's gonna be a little prick here, Ricky."

Ricky says, "'Sides you?"

The same joke everyday, and this is the last time. Silence. Ray-Ray begins to sweat. He says, "Are you sure?"

Ricky nods.

Ray-Ray asks, "Want me to get your mom?"

"She knows," Ricky says. "We talked."

"She don't want to hold your hand?"

"Fuck you," Ricky says. A long breath. "Don't make this hard."

It already is, Ray-Ray thinks. And suddenly he understands Claire's absence. It would be one thing to be present at your son's death, and quite another to be there for his killing.

Ray-Ray finds a vein in his cousin's neck—as is true of his arms, the veins in his legs have long-since collapsed—and injects the heroin. Afterwards, Ray-Ray draws up more of the junk and injects Ricky again. He does it a third time. If he's going to do this, he's going to do it right.

He looks away to pick up the spoon and the tar, and out of the corner of his eyes he sees Ricky shudder, once, and then sigh. Trying not to look at the body, Ray-Ray cleans up the nightstand—later that night he'll throw all the paraphernalia and shit into the river to have it out of his life—and leaves the room. He goes to tell his Aunt Claire. The whole time—even holding her as her whole body shakes—he doesn't let himself feel. He doesn't let himself feel until much later, and what he feels then is not so much rage or even sorrow as it is an emptiness that swells up inside of him until it's bigger than his heart, bigger than all of him, bigger than the whole damn city and everyone in it.

Ray-Ray never talks about the specifics of Ricky's death—not to anyone—but when anybody asks if at least it had been peaceful, Ray-Ray always replies, "Not for me it wasn't. Not for me."

Dujuan's dreams turn chaotic. He's never before thought much about dreams, except to relish and wait impatiently for the sexual ones. Sometimes he tries, generally unsuccessfully, to call them into being by fantasizing as he falls asleep or by watching pornography at a friend's house then coming home to bed, holding the images of sex fresh at the front of his mind. He thinks also, though only a little, about his occasional nightmares. Or rather he doesn't *think* about them so much as he attempts, again generally unsuccessfully, to banish them. But both his sexual dreams and his nightmares are rare enough, and of slight enough importance to him, that they don't intrude on his life. Now, though, dreams take over his sleep and invade his waking hours. Images rise up to take hold of his mind, images he isn't able to later shake, even all through the day.

Often in these dreams Shameka stands before him,

staring. Other times she chases him, hunts him from room to room in their home, then house to house and block to block in the city. She always finds him, and she always moves in to kill him.

The woman at the bus stop, too, enters his dreams, and she, too chases him. These dreams always end at the river, and end with her, too, moving in for the kill.

The dreams, whether of Shameka or Malia (he had gotten her name from her wallet), always end with him forcing himself to the surface of the dream. The last moments of these dreams feel each time as he felt once as a child, when he had nearly drowned. While swimming at a public pool, a much larger child had pushed him under and held him for as long as the older child could hold his breath. Dujuan had thought he was going to die. Finally the other swam away, and Dujuan burst toward the surface, knowing he could never make it the impossibly far distance of just a few feet. He exploded into the air, and let out his breath with a sob. So, too, with these dreams. Each night an act of will brings the emotions of the dream to the surface, compresses them and short-circuits them with a rush.

Though he awakens frightened from these dreams he is able each time to fall quickly back to sleep. Then more dreams come, consisting of confusing jumbles of images he tries to force his way through: coffins with no bottoms that open into subterranean worlds, cars with no engines, looming buildings that threaten to collapse in front or on top of him. His brother Boo appears in many of these dreams, saying words Dujuan can't understand, or understanding, can't remember. These dreams, too, all end the same way, at the same place, with Dujuan standing at the river that flows through the center of the city. Sometimes Boo is with him, and sometimes not. But always standing next to him is the woman from the bus stop.

Dujuan does something he has never done before: he goes by himself to the river. He'd been there plenty as a kid, to fish with friends under one of the bridges, though they knew even then not to eat the fish. Sometimes they'd waded in the shallows. Occasionally in high school he'd come down to the wreckage of the amusement park with a girlfriend and a bag of weed to stay till three or four in the morning. But he'd never been here by himself.

He comes at night, to the opposite bank from the ruins of the amusement park. He brings his father's gun. Many times since the night the hammer fell on an empty chamber he's put the gun to his head, but never again has he pulled the trigger. He wonders whether tonight he brought the gun to shoot himself or to protect himself should something move in the bushes. Perhaps he brought it to fend off the dreams.

Beyond the sickly yellow cone of his dying flashlight's beam is a different sort of dark than he's used to inside a building or on the street, or even the sort of dark he'd experienced here with a girlfriend. The dark now is deeper, more hollow and rounded, more resonant, layered, less static.

He hears a skittering in the bushes, and touches the gun he carries in his waistband. And now a sound from another direction, followed by a fluttering sound he thinks must be a startled bird.

He flicks off the flashlight and freezes in place. His heart seems to stop, and when it resumes he feels blood pulse in his neck and deep in his ears. He looks around, but sees nothing in the dark. He listens. Still nothing. In the distance the river. His shoulders hunch and his legs tighten.

He inhales deeply, yet slowly and quietly. He smells nothing. That's good. He can continue; he smells no danger.

He flicks back on the flashlight and continues down a small path toward the river. He's thankful for what he has come to know is an uncommon—a strange—sense of smell, otherwise he would still be frightened.

Dujuan's earliest memory was the smell of danger. He was five, and holding his brother's hand, standing at the intersection of two busy streets, waiting for the light to turn green. That's when he smelled it, strong, sour, bitter. He recoiled from the smell, and in stepping back pulled Boo's hand hard enough to make him, too, step away from the street. The smell became more intense, and he retreated again. Then suddenly the smell vanished, and in that moment, one he will never forget, a bus cut the corner too tight: with the growl of a diesel engine revving from a downshift, the machine drove where they had just stood. They'd looked at each other, and Dujuan'd begun to cry.

He didn't make the connection right then between the smell and the danger. It took years before that connection filtered through his body to become conscious, years of sporadic reinforcement: a subtle whiff before falling on ice, a stronger smell before getting hit hard in basketball, a stench he somehow ignored before being beaten in an alley. And there'd never been a moment when he'd said to himself, "This smell means danger." Instead he'd experienced a gradual, embodied movement back to where he'd been at the beginning—a physical recoil from something that stank—a slow training of his mind by his body to pay attention. And so he learned. More and more he began to move with the smell, before the danger became obvious, before it became unavoidable.

He never told anyone about his sense of smell, at first because he thought it normal—something everyone experienced yet rarely talked about—like hiccups or hunger pangs or occasional rage. Later, when he realized not everyone could smell danger, he didn't talk about it for fear others would think him strange, or even that they would try to convince him that what he experienced wasn't real. And later still he didn't talk about it because in time people began to notice he didn't get hit so often, and so they started to follow his lead. After that he never even considered talking about it, because he realized that with this knowledge comes power. And when you've got power, he'd known even when he was young, nothing much else matters.

He reaches the river, uses the flashlight to find a comfortable rock, sits, and turns off the light.

He thinks maybe he should have killed that woman at the bus stop. Maybe he still will. Maybe then the dreams will stop.

He's never killed anyone before, but this might be the time to start. She'd had no right to compare him to the people at Vexcorp. She'd never been poor a day in her life, and she'd never had to watch her sister die. She has no idea what he has suffered. She has no business judging him, and no business invading his dreams.

The moon comes out. It shines off the river, broken flickers of light against the empty black of the water.

I'm not like that, he thinks. *I've got nothing in common with rich people. I wish I did.*

He could see himself in an office like he's seen in movies, with carpeting and a view and private secretaries. He'd sit behind his desk and not lift a fucking finger. He wouldn't have to: money would roll in no matter what he did or didn't do. And if somebody crossed him, pfft—he snaps his fingers—the cops would take care of it.

Dujuan had once heard that justice is blind, that the rich and the poor both go to jail for stealing a loaf of bread. He thought that was bullshit at the time, and he thinks it's bullshit now. The rich don't go to jail for nothing.

The longer he sits, the more angry he becomes. Maybe he should just pop her tonight. Walk up, put the gun in the center of her forehead, and . . . No, not like that. Because in all truth he *isn't* like them. He would never do to her what the others had done to Shameka. She couldn't know that she was going to die. It's okay to let someone know you're going to beat the hell out of him, but if you're really going to kill someone, you need to at least let them die unafraid. It would be better if he came up behind her, put the gun, already cocked, behind her ear, and then did it. Or maybe find some way to make her feel safe before killing her. He would give that much to anyone.

He's glad he hasn't been able to kill himself. It's stupid and pointless to aim a gun at yourself when so many others already line up to do it for you: cops, teachers, bosses, all out to get you, all gunning you down with bullets and insults and orders and condescension. It's better, he thinks, to turn the gun around.

He reaches to touch the cool stones beside him, then the soil beneath. It, too, is cool, and gritty between his fingers.

Suddenly he's scared again. This time not of the night or the bushes or the river or the dark, but of himself. He's thought about killing people before, but it's never felt this good. And that scares him. He needs to talk to Boo. Boo will know what to do. He always does. He will know how to deal with her, and how to deal with the tangles he feels inside.

The river glistens in front of him. Something jumps in the middle, and Dujuan jumps, too, at the sound. A fish, he thinks. He hears crickets and other bugs singing. The sounds of the river and the trees surrounding it become slightly more comfortable, though still foreign. He thinks that someday he might have to come back.

∼

Dear Anthony,

Thank you so much for those three telephone conversations this past month. It makes me so happy to talk with you. And I haven't laughed that hard and that easily for years. The only problem is that now I miss you more than ever. But at least I know it's you I miss, and not my memories of you.

I want to see you! I love you,

Malia

∼

Malia had been asleep, but now she is awake. Oftentimes these days she awakens with a start and reaches for the light, seeing in her mind the image of the men from the bus stop. But this night she isn't afraid.

Nights like tonight, nights she feels safe, she loves the warm, settled feeling of her arms and legs leaden with sleep, her blood flowing like honey. She loves especially that slow dissolution of thoughts that comes as she drifts, and their just-as-gradual reclarification on awakening.

She's at her parents'. It's Friday night. She'd arrived late, after everyone else had gone to bed. She'd fallen asleep quickly, and now she looks at the clock on her headboard. The clock has been in her room since she was a child. She sees it's well past two.

Her door is open, and she sees a light on elsewhere in the house, probably in the kitchen. She thought she'd turned it off, but perhaps she hadn't. She lies languid for several moments before gathering the energy to get up to turn off the light.

She staggers to the doorway and makes her way, a little more steadily now, down the hall to the kitchen.

Her mother sits at the table, drinking tea. "Oh," her mother says, "I hope I didn't wake you."

"No, I had to get up anyway," Malia replies, looking around, blinking, at the kitchen counters. She spies a box of cereal. After a moment's hesitation, she says, "I was getting up to have a snack."

Both women smile at the lie.

Malia hears her father's light snores from down the hallway to her parents' bedroom. She likes the sound of his breathing. She fixes the cereal and sits down.

Her mother says, "I'm glad you got up."

"Me too."

Both of the women are silent for a moment, before Malia asks, "So why are you up?"

"Couldn't sleep."

"Duh, "Malia says, laughing. "Why not?"

Her mother looks at her tea in front of her, then says, "I went to the doctor. Got biopsies last week. They came back." She shakes her head slightly. "It's not good."

Malia feels bad for having laughed. She hears her voice say, "Oh, no."

"It's not that bad."

"Lymphoma?"

"I've been reading, you know. And I've got better than a

fifty percent chance of making at least five years."

"So a fifty percent chance of . . ."

Neither says anything for a very long time, before her mother says, "I guess it depends on where you put your focus."

"Does Dad know?"

"Of course. Do you think I could hide something from him? I didn't have to say a word."

Another silence. One of their cats wanders in from the living room.

Malia says, "When did you find out?"

"Wednesday." A pause before she answers the question Malia would never have asked, because to do so would have shifted the emphasis from her mother to herself. "I wanted to tell you in person." Another pause, then, "I knew if I got up, you would know and get up, too. Then we could talk."

"Did you tell Robin?"

"Not yet. But she knows, too."

"Not much gets by her." Malia looks away, then back at her mother.

Her mother says, "Don't worry. I'm not going anywhere. Your dad's got too much work to be doing it by himself. I can't die."

There it is. She said it. The word can no longer be taken back. It's in the room, almost taking on physical form.

Malia isn't going to cry. Not now. She can't, for the same reason she wouldn't have asked why her mother didn't tell her sooner. She knows if she cries her mother will comfort her. Later she will cry, and later her mother will comfort her. But now she folds her hands in front of her, and, flesh of her mother, says, "Okay, what can I do? How do you want me to help?"

"I don't know yet how I want to handle it," her mother says. "I need to let it settle in. When the time comes, I'm sure we'll all know what to do."

⊕

The drive to the prison is long. Always before, Dujuan had accepted Boo's distance from home as the result of some stupid bureaucratic decision—boiling down to bad luck—but today it begins to dawn on him that there might be more to it. Boo could just as easily have been put into a closer prison, but maybe the reason he was so far away, Dujuan thinks, is to make it more difficult on him. Perhaps Boo's placement is part of a program to tear apart their family. Of course he isn't so paranoid as to believe the penal system has it out for Boo and Boo alone, or more generally for their family—the bureaucrats undoubtedly never think about Boo at all—but he does believe conscious decisions are made to locate prisoners far from their homes. The reason? Just to fuck things up.

Contrary to what he would have expected, this realization doesn't make Dujuan overtly angry. Nor does he just accept it with a shrug. Instead, and this is part of the new Dujuan he feels beginning to emerge, he drops the information deep inside where he can digest it, and where eventually he can use it for fuel. But fuel for what? That's the question he's driving up to find out.

Ray-Ray and Simon ride along. Some visits they go inside with him, or with him and the rest of his family, but today Dujuan said he wanted to go in alone. They came along for company, and because it was something to do. They'll stay at a pizza place while Dujuan goes inside.

They make the long drive shorter at first by lying to each other about sex.

Ray-Ray says, "Yo, Dujuan, what's up wit that light-skinned chick you used to talk to from Thirty-fourth Street? Did you ever hit that, or she still playin hard to get?"

Dujuan replies, "Of course I did. And her sister's always askin about you. I gave her yo number the last time I was there."

Ray-Ray looks at him. "I don't believe you, because she ain't called."

Dujuan says, "I ain't got no reason to lie to you about no girl, man."

Simon interjects, "Yeah, right. You know girls don't want

yo ugly ass. Give 'em my number from now on." They all laugh.

These moments usually lighten the mood. But today Dujuan can't get comfortable. Not with them or with himself. Not fully. Not even with the music. Not even when listening to Pac's *White Man's World*: "Staring at walls of Silence/Inside this cage/Where they captured all my rage and violence/In time I learned a few lessons/Never fall for riches . . ."

Always in front of him during that long drive is that last image of Shameka, thrashing, and then Malia at the bus stop, and what Malia said: "You're so much like Vexcorp, they probably don't even have to send cops down to keep you in line."

Dujuan had written a letter to Boo about what he was feeling, what he wanted to do. He knew the guards read letters, so he'd been subtle, not incriminating himself for anything, but he knew also that the guards were more interested in checking for drugs than ferreting information, and he knew Boo. Boo would understand. He was the only one who would understand. That was why Dujuan couldn't talk about this with his friends. That was why he hadn't mentioned to them his reasons for coming.

Dujuan drives. Ray-Ray rides shotgun. Simon sits in the back. The tires whine. The sun is hot through the windshield. They roll down the windows, and Dujuan listens to the wind outside.

Once, they see a deer, and later they see a dead cat and then a big dead raccoon. Many times they see ravens flying low with slow smooth beats of their wings. They don't think much about any of these, but simply let the images into their eyes and into their brains, then forget about them as the miles roll by.

There's another reason that Simon rides along, and that's to be near his father, even if they don't speak to or acknowledge each other, even if they don't see each other. Even if each doesn't know who the other is. Even if Simon only sits here in a fucking pizza parlor, four miles from the prison. At least he will be only four miles from his father.

All the stuff Simon says about his father, about not knowing where he is, about wanting to see him laugh: it's all bullshit, and Simon knows it. Simon knows exactly where he is—in the same prison as Boo. Boo told Simon that two years ago, but Simon made him promise not to tell anyone else.

Here's what Boo told Simon: when Simon's father heard his mom was pregnant he didn't run off, at least the way most people do. Instead he drove straightaway to another town, held up a jewelry store, and shot an off-duty cop working security. Years later, talking to Boo, Simon's father said he did it so the family could afford Simon, but as Simon came to understand it, all he scored was four hundred and fifty-five dollars. Simon guessed his mother knew all this, but she never talked about it. Simon often says, to himself and no one else, "What's he gonna buy me for four hundred and fifty-five fucking dollars? The man don't know shit about me, and I've never even seen his face."

Simon looks at his hands and realizes they are balled into fists. He forces them to relax. He looks to the front of the car and tries to focus on the sounds of the automobile.

Although Dujuan doesn't normally so much notice his natural surroundings, he always does notice that the approach to the prison is beautiful, all the moreso in contrast to what comes next.

The trees are deciduous, and through the seasons Dujuan has seen them tender green in spring, orange and red in the fall, and as etched skeletons tangled against a steel winter sky. He thinks that just as the prisoners are intentionally kept far from their homes, they are also kept in such a beautiful place to remind them on their way in of everything they would for a long time—perhaps forever—be missing.

The last couple of miles before the prison, the highway becomes an avenue of giant trees, tops reaching over the highway to twine together and to clash in the wind of passing trucks. Below,

impenetrable mountains of brush push against the road. Dujuan
sees sprays of white flowers he knows will later become dark clusters
of berries hanging heavy from thorny vines. He's always wondered
how the berries would taste, but has never stopped to check.

The plot for the prison had been carved out of the forest, a
huge square denuded of trees and tall bushes to maintain an open
field of fire. In the center of the square, a series of squat concrete
buildings clusters around a central mass that Dujuan's been told
contains the dreaded SHU, or Secure Housing Unit, where disfa-
vored prisoners spend months and years alone in their cells, separated from all human contact save that with guards and rare visits
from family. Boo was in the SHU for a year and a half, getting out
only a few months ago. He'd refused all visits during that time—"I
don't want Mama to see me in shackles"—and had never talked
about it. He'd been sent there for kicking a guard.

Dujuan's car is third in line to enter the check point at
the edge of the prison grounds. He hopes they won't search it. He
cleaned it out as best he could, but mistakes happen. Last year
an empty beer can in the trunk cost his neighbor Mr. Ballinger a
year's visiting privileges to his son, and three years ago Mrs. Jasper's
cousin forgot a pocketknife between the seats and was arrested for
attempting to smuggle a weapon onto the grounds.

He's second in line, and then first. The guard—a burly bald
man with at least three big sticks up his butt—asks for Dujuan's
ID, walks to the front of the car, and checks Dujuan's name against
a list of visitors approved for today's visits. He walks back to the
window, looks at Dujuan, and says, "You'll wanna pull over to the
side there, Son."

Fuck. Dujuan blames this on Malia. He knows if he
weren't so fucked up about her they wouldn't have pulled him over.
They smell his nerves. He drives to the side.

Two other guards approach. One is young, the same age as
Dujuan. The other has silver hair. He hates them both.

The younger one says, "Will you get out of the car please, sir?"

He does.

The older man says, "Why so anxious? You trying to sneak in some doobie?" He laughs to let Dujuan know it's a joke.

Dujuan doesn't think it's funny. He wants to tell the man to fuck off. He wants to kill him. He hopes they aren't going to plant anything.

The younger man says, "Would you open the back, please?"

He does that, too.

They lift the spare tire. They search the rest of the trunk. They ask him to open the rear doors, and he does. They rummage under the seats.

"You're clean," says the younger one.

"Like a boy scout," says the other. "I'll catch you next time."

Dujuan gets in the car. He turns the key in the ignition, then follows the road that skirts the prison's perimeter. A single car comes the opposite direction. It's driven by a guard. He's heard that the car circles the prison twenty-four hours per day, and that the guards who drive it carry a shotgun and sidearm within reach. If he were forced to drive in circles like that, Dujuan wonders, how long would it take him before from boredom he turned one of those guns back on himself?

To Dujuan's immediate right is a series of three tall fences: two chain-link topped with razor wire, and an electric fence between, carrying lethal voltage. The middle fence looks innocuous—slender wires on glass insulators—but signs in Spanish and English announce differently. Tall gun towers stand at intervals along the fence. Between the fence and the concrete pods that make up the prison itself is a graveled dead zone. No bushes, grasses, or even weeds grow there. Nothing. Windows narrow as arrow slits line the prison walls.

He pulls into the lot and gets out of his car. There aren't

many people today. He makes his way to the processing room. Several guards stand by, patting down visitors, making them remove their shoes and twisting them to make sure no knives are hidden in the soles, and going through women's long hair for the same reason. Guards wave him through a metal detector, and then he passes through several remote-controlled gates before finally reaching his destination.

The large room looks like nothing so much as the lunchroom from his elementary school, except with video cameras and guards. The same linoleum floor, the same cheap Formica tables and plastic chairs. He almost expects Mrs. Kupers—wearing an apron, pink floral dress, and hairnet—to enter through one of the doors carrying a green plastic tray of Chef's Surprise.

Boo arrives soon after Dujuan. He wears blue jeans and a light blue chambray shirt, as he always does.

Boo looks Dujuan over, says, "You look like shit."

"It's good to see you, too, Boo."

They briefly hug.

Dujuan says, "We gotta talk."

"I know," Boo says, "I got yo letter."

Boo hasn't seen the stars since he came to prison. Nor has he seen the moon at night. It's been years since he saw a sunrise or sunset.

For eighteen months in SHU he didn't talk to anyone who didn't wear a uniform. During that time he stopped wearing clothes. He stopped bathing until he was forcibly carried to the shower by a white-suited extraction team. He refused haircuts, but was held down and shaved. His original sentence in SHU was six months, but these refusals cost him time, and time again.

He lost his sense of taste, but ate because his body demanded. He slept away the days until one day he forgot how to sleep, and lost track of the difference between sleeping and waking. Since that time he has never been sure which is which.

In a rage, or maybe in a dream, he destroyed the television in his cell. The radio, too, he broke. He broke them because they were burrowing into his brain.

So he sat, and he thought, and he dreamed, and he couldn't tell the difference. He thought that he screamed, and thought he heard the screams of others far away. But those could have been dreams.

He read books. He was allowed one at a time. He would read it, then read it last chapter to first, then read it again. Then he would get another book. He began, naked and dreaming, to plan the revolution that would turn over everything around him, that would bring, as he called it in whispered conversations with himself, the great healing.

He was sent to SHU for kicking a guard who hit him with a baton. But Boo had done it all wrong. He remembered later that the guard had an artificial leg, which meant Boo was sent to the hole for kicking a piece of plastic. That was not a mistake he would make again.

There were others in the SHU. He'd heard of men who when they were finally dragged out balled themselves into the fetal position, too scared even to stand, and of others who bathed in shit, and still others who routinely gassed the guards—threw mixtures of piss and shit at them, hoping to hit their eyes. One killed himself by ramming his head into a wall. But Boo wasn't going to do any of that. The reason? He wasn't crazy. Others might be. But not him. He began long conversations with others who were sane through short scrawled notes secreted in the volumes of the law library—to which they could not legally be denied access—and learned that some of these men had been in solitary for more than two decades.

The men in SHU formed an odd sort of community, never meeting, yet recognizing birthdays and holy days, teaching each other about politics, meditation, spirituality. Sharing stories. One man had been inside since he was eight. Not in the SHU, of course, but in institutions. He would probably be in forever. A few of them had seen their fathers kill their mothers, or vice versa. Several had been prostituted out by their fathers, grandfathers, uncles. Nearly all had been abused, first by parents—Boo had not suffered this one—then by cops, now by guards.

Though Boo no longer knew the difference between waking and dreaming, he knew from these conversations that he wasn't crazy. He knew that the problems lay not with him.

Boo was dying of boredom. He counted the pockmarks in the cement walls of his cell. Each wall had about 13,000. The difficulty of deciding what was or wasn't a pockmark and where one began and another stopped made a more definitive accounting impossible. Yet he tried. And the more he tried, the more the pockmarks took on shapes, and had he been crazy he would have thought they formed messages to him, as cryptic yet clear as the messages in the law library. But he knew these were just pockmarks.

His room was precisely seven by eight feet, with a concrete bed, a concrete sink, and a concrete toilet. For hours he walked two and a quarter paces one direction and two and a quarter paces back. He was walking home, counting the steps and calculating how much farther he had to walk.

He did burpees—1,000 at a pop. And he did exactly 1,300 jumping jacks at a time, one for every ten pockmarks. And 1,300 sit-ups. And then he would walk some more.

As he walked he dreamed about prison, but his dreams weren't about concrete and metal and electrified fences, dog runs and mace and stun guns, wooden bullets and pepper spray. He dreamt of many things. He often remembered a little girl he saw years ago. She was eating an ice cream cone. Boo saw her from the back of a cop car, and though she never saw him, he would never forget her, because he knew he might never in his life see another little girl eat another ice cream cone. He saw his little sister before she got sick. He saw Dujuan in the rooftop garden. Boo saw the first time he spiked one of his own veins, and he saw the last. The prison that Boo dreamed of wasn't about Plexiglas, steel, panopticon designs, flailing batons, hidden shivs, smelling your own farts, masturbating while the surveillance camera records every movement. Those were just the final stages of the dream. The dream started much earlier, with where you were born, when you were born, why you were born, and most especially who you were born. This was the first part of the dream, the first part of the prison. He knew that. This was the dream—and the prison—that determined all of the others. Yet he knew also that the second and even more important part of the dream, which is to say the prison's second wall, the lethal electric fence, is erected the moment you believe that the first part of the dream is true. To turn off the electric fence—click—you have to disbelieve in the power of the first dream. You have to understand that the walls of that first prison are no more natural than the concrete walls and electric fences of the second. You have to understand that *someone* fabricates these walls, and that *someone* benefits from them, and that someone else will have to tear them down.

Boo knew all of this because he dreamed it, and if he dreamed it, it must be true. This is what Boo carried with him, concealed deep within, where not even cavity searches could reach, when finally he returned from the SHU.

The woman stands outside the closed door. She raises her hand to knock, then hesitates. There are so many reasons she doesn't want to go in. The first is that Donald, her supervisor, is a jerk, or more accurately, a leering sexist jerk. No matter how conservatively Jessica dresses, his gaze always finds her breasts, her crotch. And he makes comments. They never rise to an actionable level of sexual harassment, but they nonetheless make her uncomfortable.

Another reason she doesn't want to go in is that she's in a good mood, and Donald has a gift for reading people and saying whatever is guaranteed to make the other person feel the worst. She's not sure if this is a conscious or unconscious gift.

Yet another reason is that he's a fucking cowboy who does everything his way, breaks rules just for the heck of it, and seems to know how to play both supervisors and "inferiors"—as he calls them—well enough to always get away with it.

Like now. He's gotten her to play along. And it looks like he's going to get away with it again. The phone and mail intercepts have been illegal all along, but they seem to have paid off.

That should make her happy—one step closer to catching the bad guys, or in this case, bad girl—but it doesn't.

She knocks.

She hears a voice say, "Enter."

She walks into Donald's office. She sits.

The man doesn't say anything, for a time doesn't even look up from his paperwork.

The woman says, "You were right about the phone taps and mail intercepts, sir. She's called him several times."

"Who is him?

"Malia Jenning's ex-boyfriend, sir."

"Wonderful," he says. "Do we know where she is?"

"Not yet, sir. But we know she wants to see him."

Donald smiles through thin lips, then says, "We've finally got her where we want her. We're going to nail that fucking bitch to the wall." He seems to notice Jessica wince, seems to remember she always winces when he says the word bitch. *He says, "Nothing personal."*

Jessica asks, "What do we do now?"

"Wait," Donald says. "We wait."

When Dujuan picks up Ray-Ray and Simon after his visit with Boo, something has changed about his face, his demeanor. *It's like he saw a ghost,* Ray-Ray thinks. Dujuan is quiet, and seems near tears. He doesn't drive on the way home, but rides in the passenger seat, chain-smoking and flicking burning ashes out the window.

Simon asks, "So?"

Ray-Ray looks sidelong at Dujuan. Dujuan blows smoke toward the cracked window. It swirls out.

Simon asks, "What did you talk about?"

"Don't be an asshole," Ray-Ray interjects. "Let him be."

"No, it's okay," says Dujuan.

Then nothing. Simon leans up between the seats, looking back and forth between Ray-Ray and Dujuan like a friendly dog. All he needs is a long tongue and a doggie grin. He fixes on Dujuan expectantly.

"We talked about prison."

"And. . . ?"

"And we talked about prison. What it is. Who's in there."

Even out of the corner of his eyes, Ray-Ray can see Simon flinch at this latter. He can also see that Dujuan doesn't notice.

Dujuan takes another drag on his cigarette. He says, "And we talked about gettin out."

Simon says, surprised, "Boo's gettin out?"

Simon can be so stupid, Ray-Ray thinks. *It's probably all the drugs.*

Once again, Dujuan doesn't say anything for a long time, and when at last he does, Ray-Ray can barely hear him. He says, "No, I am."

Dear Anthony,

I never told you how I got away the day that Robin got killed. One of the things both Robin and I learned, being on the run, was to always have escape routes. This was true wherever we lived, and it was true wherever we went: to grocery stores, restaurants, or anywhere. Always—ALWAYS—find the exits.

We were renting a small farmhouse in the country. We'd been there for several months. It had a pasture on one side and a forest on the other. The forest was extremely dense, with game trails that literally forced you to crawl. These game trails led quickly to a river. Our primary escape plan consisted of going into the cellar and out the cellar door—think the Kansas scenes in Wizard of Oz for a visual—then running just a few sheltered steps toward a ditch we'd dug and covered over. We'd crawl in this ditch for maybe sixty feet, then crawl game trails another fifty yards to the river.

Digging and disguising the ditch took a lot of effort, but we didn't so much mind doing it since we knew our lives might depend on it.

It ends up they didn't. One day soon after we finished digging I was doing laundry and noticed a tiny crack between a set of wooden shelves and the wall. I'd always presumed the shelves were built-in, but they weren't, and when I pulled them out I discovered a closet-sized room behind, underneath the landing on the stairs to the second floor. It wasn't precisely a secret room. More likely whoever put in the laundry room couldn't figure out what to do with this half-height space, so they covered the entrance with shelves.

We extended the wall just a little to get rid of the crack I'd seen in the first place, then attached L-brackets to the back of the shelf assembly and made screw-holes in the floor and ceiling so we could lock the shelves in place from the inside and hope anyone outside would think it was bolted to the wall.

It worked perfectly, except for the most important part: Robin was dead.

part four

in the dirt outside.

I heard the FBI tromping around the house, heard them cursing me, heard them gloating over killing Robin, heard them calling her names that would have appalled and horrified their own mothers. And I heard them vowing to kill me for making fools of them.

But I never heard them pulling down the bookshelves.

I waited in there until I thought it was safe, then made my way to that original ditch and down that toward the river. I dug up some cash we'd stashed and tried to start over.

I'm tired of running. I want to fight back.

Love,

Malia   ∼

It is two months later. It is Friday evening. Malia works at her desk. It is, as always, covered with documents. The thick Vexcorp folder she borrowed from Dennis sits on one corner. The desk no longer squats against a wall, but has been turned so Malia can face the door. This doesn't stop her from jumping in fright when the door bursts open and Dennis rushes in.

Before he can say anything, Malia says, smiling, "No, Dennis, no bugs. I swept last week and found one, so I asked Wayne to come in last night and check the suite. He found a couple more: one in the lobby and one in your office, but none in any of the others."

Dennis doesn't say anything.

Malia says, "I'm sure the one last week was because of the *60 Minutes* gig."

He nods, then plops himself into the chair nearest her desk.

Malia asks, "Did you finalize the schedule with them?"

"They're talking to me and the locals over the weekend and then Vexcorp people on Monday."

"Knock em dead."

"Will you be available this weekend, in case they want to talk to you?"

"I'm going to my parents'. If you need me, call and I'll be happy to drive down."

Neither speaks. Malia knows what's going to come next: a continuation of the nonconversation they've been having since the two began working together. He's going to tell her to temper her message.

And here it comes, right on schedule. He says, "If you talk to them, no doom and gloom, okay?"

"Don't tell me what to say."

"I didn't mean—"

"There's no way you can candy-coat telling me what to say."

"This is really important to me."

Malia doesn't want to waste more energy fighting this battle. Not with Dennis. Not right now. She says, "Okay. This is your event. You tell me what to say and I'll say it."

He looks at her, dubious.

She says, "Really."

He shakes his head. "No. Say whatever you want." A slight pause. "Just please don't talk about revolution."

Malia nods, "Sure, great. Whatever."

"And no anger."

"No problem."

"And no anti-corporate stuff. Don't jump to the larger pic-ture. The only way they'll actually air the thing is if we present this as a unique problem to which we've found a unique solution that will make everyone uniquely happy."

"Jesus Christ. You want to just hand me a written script? Can I at least use the phrase *the collapse of industrial civilization*?"

"I thought no doom and gloom."

"That ain't gloom, buddy. That's our only hope."

He stares at her intently, and finally says, "You really don't think we'll pull our fat out of the fire, do you?"

"Of course not. The ones running the show are psychopaths—"

"Don't say that!"

"What?"

"To *60 Minutes*. They'll think we're lunatics."

"Thank you very much."

He looks to the side, and considers for a moment.

"Your rhetoric is so polarizing."

"The polarity already exists," she says. "I'm not the one poisoning the river."

"How do people respond when you talk this way?"

"They know what I'm talking about."

"Well, I don't like it."

Malia doesn't say anything. She doesn't much care anymore whether Dennis likes what she says. She's as tired of fighting her allies as she is her enemies.

Dennis looks at the documents on her desk. He points and asks, "Another appeal?"

Malia nods. "Another late night."

There's a long silence before Dennis comments, "Have I told you how sorry I am I didn't walk you to the bus that night?"

"It's okay."

"When was that, two months ago?"

"Seven weeks, three days," she looks at her watch, then continues, "Twenty-two hours, and fifteen minutes."

Neither speaks, until Dennis asks, "How are you doing with all that?"

"Nights are the worst. I still check my closets and under my bed. I heard someone call it 'the democracy of fear.' Anywhere in the world, any woman can be walking down any street, and if she hears footsteps behind her, she has reason to be afraid. Anywhere. Everywhere. I always thought if I ignored the fear hard enough, nothing would happen to me. I was wrong."

"So how is the walking to the bus thing these days?"

She shrugs.

"Have you seen them?"

"No." Malia pauses, then says, "And . . . I bought this." She opens the drawer of her desk and pulls out a small pistol. It gleams under the office's fluorescent lights.

Dennis leans away. "Holy shit. Is it loaded?"

"Of course."

"Have you fired it?"

"At my parents'." She looks at the gun, then back at Dennis. "This is a good thing."

"I can't picture you firing a gun."

"I grew up on a farm." She hesitates, then continues, "But to be honest I couldn't see me picking up a handgun either. Until the democracy of fear changed my vision." Another hesitation before she says, "And . . . when the revolution does come, I want to be prepared."

Dennis says, emphatically, "No. No. That's not right."

"Dennis, get serious. We both know the only reason you and I are alive is that the other side is winning. It's part of an unspoken agreement. We don't threaten their profits, and they don't threaten us. If we broke our part of the bargain, we'd be dead in no time."

"You believe that?"

Malia is silent, then begins to speak, at first slowly, and then rapid fire: "Salvador Allende. Tupac Amaru. Death squads in Honduras, El Salvador, Chile. Colombia. Peru. Haiti. Mexico. Torture squads. Assassination Programs. The Phoenix Program. Patrice Lamumba. Arbenz. Do you want me to keep going?" She looks around, wildly, at the posters on the wall, and at the walls themselves. Then she looks back to Dennis, and says, quietly, "Of course my talk of revolution is just that. The gun stays in my desk all day, and in my pocket when I walk to and from the bus." Another pause, before she says, intently, "You don't know how frightened I get. All the time. Every moment. Every day."

"Of the thugs?"

"Are you even listening, Dennis? I'm frightened of everything I talk about. What I think about. What I know. What I understand. All the shit that goes on." She stops and puts her hand up, palm facing Dennis, then says, only slightly condescendingly, "Don't worry. I won't mention this to *60 Minutes*."

Neither says anything.

Finally, Malia continues, quietly, "You know, I'm really scared . . ."

Dennis responds, impatiently, "I don't get it."

Malia shakes her head. She knows Dennis is not naturally this obtuse. She says, "You're not helping at all. I'm trying to talk here. About something important."

"Talk?"

"About issues, about the future. About actions that might actually stop the poisonings . . . That might actually start to shut down the machine."

"The machine."

She believes Dennis creates this artificial stupidity to keep himself from noticing anything that will upset his worldview. She wonders at the ubiquity of this stupidity, which she knows extends to herself as well. To everyone. She thinks but does not say, *How else do we explain the absurdity of poisoning children for profit? Of allowing children to be poisoned? If a foreign government did this to us, we'd rise up in a flash. But since we pledge allegiance to this enemy, we go along.* She continues, "But what's worse is how scared I am of what will happen if we continue to not act. Sometimes I feel like a part of me is missing." She points to the poster of the mother grizzly. "If someone were killing the little grizzly cubs, I don't think she'd philosophize her way to inaction. She would just know what to do." There's a long pause before she says, "Perhaps we think we have too much to lose."

Another pause, before Dennis says, surprisingly thoughtfully, "Maybe that's what fear is."

"What?"

"The belief we have something to lose."

Malia studies him. She's never heard him speak so seriously. Then she watches his face as he suddenly—though on a level he could never be aware of—becomes frightened by his own candor. His eyes flicker, first to the left and then up as his mind races to find a way to change the subject. Finally he finds one, a familiar one, a friendly one. He shifts the focus to himself. He asks, "Do you still respect me? Even though I'm not so radical as you?"

She, too, falls into a familiar role, and begins to take care of his feelings, thus letting both him and her step away from the implications of her line of thought. She says, "I wasn't talking about you. Everything is so fucked up that anything we do helps. I haven't the enthusiasm or patience—or faith—to get *60 Minutes* here. And if that saves the life of one kid . . ."

He nods, safe because of his diffusion of the conversation's energy.

Malia knows better than to try to reignite their talk. She asks, "What are you doing tonight?"

"I haven't decided. I do know I'm gonna crash early. I've got to meet their plane at 7:00 in the morning."

"Are you bringing them to the office tomorrow?"

"I don't think so. We're going to take a field trip to the river."

After a moment, Malia says, "Don't forget the marshmallows . . ."

"Huh?"

"To roast if the river catches fire."

"Gotcha."

With that, Dennis stands, stretches, and walks out. Malia, too, stands and stretches. She hears the front office door open and shut. As she sits back down, she notices the Vexcorp file still on her desk. She snatches it up and runs out the front door, hoping to catch Dennis before he leaves. But he's gone, so she comes back inside to call him. His cell phone is off so she leaves a message. Malia tells him not to worry if he can't find the file. She'll leave it on the corner of her desk so he can pick it up if she leaves before he gets back. She wishes him luck for the next day.

She hangs up the telephone and turns to look at the poster of the grizzly. Malia wishes she were as strong as she knows the bear to be.

Dennis orders another beer, his third, or maybe his fourth, he can't remember. The woman who brings his beer—a Hope Street Bitter—is pretty, and getting prettier by the glass. Her hair is blonde, in a muddy sort of way, and she has a round face and a lot of meat on her bones. Her steel-gray eyes are soft despite their color.

He comes here often. The Marshlands, it's called. An environmentally-friendly bar where friendly environmentalists come to get tanked. Dennis brought Malia here once, back when they were dating. She'd hated it. He'd found that hard to believe: what's there to hate? The place has floors made of recycled tires and walls of recycled cardboard pressed into a facsimile of wood. A copy of the book *Clearcut* is on the bar, and he'd even seen copies of the magazine *Live Wild or Die* floating around the tables. He'd figured especially this latter would have made her happy. But she'd still hated it. Too loud, she'd said. And there'd been something else . . . His mind crawls this way and that as he tries to recall what it was. Oh, yeah, she doesn't drink. And she doesn't like being around people who do.

The waitress with round bosom and rounder bottom comes by, and suddenly Dennis remembers it hasn't been three or four beers, but instead six. Six delightful Hope Street Bitters. Or maybe, now that he thinks about it again, seven. He's also working on the biggest goddamn pile of French fries he's ever seen. He asks for another bowl of ketchup.

The waitress leaves, and Dennis thinks again about Malia. Her problem, it occurs to him, is that she doesn't know when to give up. For all her talk about "shutting down the machine," it seems to have escaped her that the machine has already won.

It's everywhere. She herself is a creation of the machine. We're all stamped from the same mold. Oh, some of us get a little rough around the edges, but we're still cogs, and we still push the machine forward. It's inescapable. It's who we are. It's what we are. Even the parts in seeming opposition—like Malia, like himself to a lesser degree—are necessary to the machine's functioning, governors to keep it from spinning into pieces, or better, valves to let off steam and keep the thing from exploding. Far from our efforts grinding it to a halt, he thinks, particularly proud of the lucidity the alcohol seems to enable—*in vino veritas*—these dissenting efforts do worse than nothing: worse even than keeping the machine intact, they actually give the machine energy. How else, if he is honest, can he explain environmentalism being used to sell beer, or to sell anything?

No matter how he tries, he can't get Malia to realize the revolution is long-since over, and that we lost without ever firing a shot. He can't get her to see that all there is left for us to do—those of us who even care—is to salve our consciences by "doing the right thing," and winning whatever victories we can, meaningless though they may ultimately be. Perhaps the only honorable thing to do, he reasons, is to hold the hands of the dying and to sputter our rage at those who are killing us all. And perhaps the only sane way to be is realistic, which means to realize it's too late to fundamentally change anything. It's probably always been too late. Best, then, of course, to simply take care of one's own.

The ketchup arrives, and Dennis looks deep into the waitress's eyes. She holds his glance for a moment, and Dennis considers moving the conversation beyond food and drink. He wonders if she would come home with him. She turns away.

Dennis's thoughts, too, turn away, back to Malia, and he pictures her as he last saw her, holding her gun, under her precious posters, Che Guevara looking over one shoulder, the bear over the other. He realizes that even more than love he feels pity for her, because she seems incapable of internalizing the messages of even those posters. What happened to Che? And what happens to "problem bears," to every grizzly who "fights back"? For all Malia's fancy listing of people and groups who've been gunned down for opposing the machine, Dennis is afraid she still doesn't get it. He wishes that right now she were sitting across from him so he could throw her words back at her, ask her if deep inside she understands what happens to people who don't play by the system's rules. He would watch her eyes as he asked, "Does the word *crucifixion* mean anything to you?" *Oh, she says she understands,* he thinks as he takes another sip of Hope Street Bitter, *but if she really did, she'd never step outside the lines.*

Malia doesn't notice when someone opens the Council's outer door. Nor does she notice when someone makes his way through the lobby. She doesn't notice when a man quietly pushes open the door to her office and steps inside. She doesn't notice him until he has taken two steps—cautious and naturally quiet—into the room. He makes a small noise in his throat.

She looks up, gasps, opens the drawer, and grasps her pistol. It's the man from the bus stop. The first one who had approached her. She aims at his body. She says, "You."

"Me."

"Get out."

"I came—" he says.

"Get out!" she says again.

He finishes his sentence, "—to apologize."

She says, "Apology accepted. Now get the hell out."

He says, "You right."

"I'm glad. Now how many times do I have to say it?—"

"I talked to my brother—" he says, and steps further into the room, slowly, non-menacingly.

She asks, "What are you doing?"

"—up at the pen," he says.

"—Why—"

"—My older brother—"

"Leave," she says.

The man points at the pistol. "You should flick off the safety—"

She looks down for a moment, then back up to him.

He continues, "—before you use that. It's the—"

She cuts him off. "I know where it is." She flicks off the safety.

He says, "You can shoot me now."

"What do you want?

"I want to tell you I'm sorry."

"You did that."

"I never told any bitch I'm sorry."

She glares at him, says, "You still haven't. I'm not a bitch."

Silence. He nods thoughtfully, then says, "You right. I never told a woman I'm sorry."

"It's a good thing to do."

"Except my mom," he says.

"That's a good place to start."

He continues, "And my little sister."

"Did you beat her, too?"

"She dead," he says. He pauses, then continues, "I'm sorry I hit you. And just so you know, we never would have . . ."

"Raped me?"

"No, never. We just fuckin wit you."

She looks at him, not speaking.

"But I'm done wit dat shit." Another long pause before he says, "My brother told me you were right."

She asks, "Why is he in the pen?"

"Sold weed to police." A slight hesitation, then, "Not the brightest in the world."

"How long?"

"Strike three, you know what I'm sayin?"

There's a silence, before she says, "Sit down."

He sits—cautiously, Malia thinks, or perhaps just smoothly. His movements are fluid, like tall grass in the wind. Malia keeps the gun in her hand, but folds her hands on the desk. The gun no longer points in his direction.

He says, "My name is Dujuan."

She asks, "How'd you find me?"

"Yo wallet," Dujuan says, and pulls it from his shirt pocket. He throws it on the desk. "Yo money is all there. Ray-Ray's sorry, too, and Simon."

"What's this about?"

It's a long time before Dujuan speaks. Then he starts, haltingly, picking up speed as he continues, "I was tellin my brother about what happened, what we did. And, you know, we done that before, I'm not gonna lie to you, we do it all the time, but I told him what you said, about, about us being like Vexcorp . . . An he said you were right. My sister's dead, see. My little sister. And Ray-Ray's cousin. They both died these past two years, and it's fuckin me up, you know what I'm sayin?"

She has no response.

He continues, "People say 'Quit wastin yo life. Get over it.' They tell me to get a fuckin job at WalMart, or they say, 'Vexcorp's hirin, go there.' I don't want that. I don't know what I want. But I know that's not what I want. And I know these fuckers are so scandalous I just want to strap up and lay waste to every motherfucker in the place, you know what I'm sayin? It's not just my sister, and it's not just Ray-Ray's cousin. It goes back way before they died. All the shit just fucks wit me sometimes, and Ray-Ray, and Simon, too, and all the rest of us."

She stares at his face, his active eyes, dark hair. She doesn't think she wants to know where this is headed.

He looks past her a moment, then meets her eyes. She looks away, and he says, "Money's good when you have it . . . An sometimes it feels good to hit somebody . . . An when you get that feelin, it don't wanna to let you go. I never thought about Vexcorp or anything but that feelin, even after my sister died, especially after my sister died. Her name was Shameka. I never thought about it at all, till you said that."

Malia definitely doesn't want to know where this is headed.

She wants to tell him to leave, so she can go back to tearing apart environmental impact statements, go back to filing appeals.

Dujuan pauses, waits for her to look at him. Then, "So I talked to my brother, and he's been talkin to people up there, people been there twenty years, thirty years, the POWs, like this one guy been there twenty years for killin a cop when he wasn't even in the state. And he said you were right. They all said you were right. You put a bunch of explosives on a table, and light a match, and then poof, you got nothin but a burn mark on your table and a stink in your house. That's what my brother said. He said you gotta to be specific. He said you put that same stuff behind a bullet, then you aim it, and then you got somethin. You got to aim yo anger, he said, and aim it at the right places, the right people."

He looks at her searchingly.

Why doesn't he leave? she thinks. *Why don't I ask him to leave?*

He says, "My sister died of cancer."

"Oh."

"And Ray-Ray's cousin."

"Oh."

"My sister was twelve. My dad died of it, too, but I never saw him much. You wouldn't believe all the people I know. Asthma, they can't breathe. Leukemia. Hodgkin's. I learned all those words before I learned to talk regular."

Malia wishes Dennis were here. He would know how to deflect the conversation, dispel this man's energy.

He says, "When you said you worked to stop cancer, until then I didn't think anybody gave a goddamn. Except my mother . . . Ray-Ray's aunt . . . But somebody on the other side. Somebody rich."

On the other side, she thinks, *rich.*

He says, "I didn't understand right then. That's why I'm sorry."

She says, "You know, *60 Minutes* is going to be here tomorrow. Do you want to talk to them?"

Dujuan looks at her quizzically. "Why?"

"Tell your story."

"What they gonna do?"

"Let everybody know."

"And?"

She leans forward. She doesn't understand the question. Once again, she doesn't want to. She says, "And then everybody will know."

"Yeah. And?"

"And what?"

"What happens then?"

A voice inside of her says, *A few people get outraged, at least until the next commercial.*

Dujuan says, "Fuck em."

She blinks and stares at him, then hears her voice ask, as if her lips and tongue and throat had a will all their own: "What are you going to do?'

He says, "It's done."

She continues to stare. *Please go*, her mind says, but her mouth won't say it.

He says, "I was thinkin, we talk about Vexcorp and all like they real, and people talk about them like they was people, but they not. They nothin. They don't exist cept we make believe. So I got to thinkin there's got to be somebody pullin strings. And the ones pullin strings don't fight face to face. They punks. And if they punks they need to be hurt. That's the only way you deal with punks. Punks don't learn any other way."

Finally Malia is able to make herself say, "I don't know what you're talking about."

He spits, "What, now you so damn stupid you can't make the connection? I already told you my sister died of cancer. What part of punk don't you understand?" He is silent for a moment, and leans close across the desk. He continues, "I ain't stupid. I'm poor. There's a difference. I can read, I can look up in a library where somebody lives. We planned it all out. We drove up there . . ."

She closes her eyes.

Dujuan leans back, and says, "He's in the trunk."

"Who," she says. Not a question. A statement.

"The punk."

"What punk?"

"Funny," Dujuan says. "I had you pegged for being smart. Even you don't fuckin get it, do you?"

Malia doesn't want to think about it. She wants nothing more than for this man to go away.

This is not why Jessica had joined the bureau. Sure, this woman was, according to at least one definition, one of the bad guys she'd signed on to put away. But somewhere along the line things had gotten far more complex and troubling than she'd ever imagined they could. She remembered the case when things began to change for her, and it hadn't even been a federal case: it was some small-town murder charge she'd read about on the Internet. Some thirty-year-old guy had walked into an older man's house, shot him in the chest, held the man's wife and son at gunpoint till the older man died, then set the gun down, walked to his parents', and surrendered to police. Simple, right? But then it came out that in his childhood and adolescence, the younger man had for years been sexually abused by the older man. There's one layer of complexity. And the younger man had killed the older man when he discovered the older man was abusing someone new. There's another layer of complexity. More abuse victims came forward: twelve in this town of several thousand. The man had coached Little League, led Boy Scouts. You want more complexity (or maybe now more simplicity)? The old man's ex-wife contributed to the young man's legal defense fund, and the old man's now-widow and son—who both had been forced to watch the old man die—spoke out in defense of the young man. And the district attorney—elected on a tough-on-crime campaign, and who saw this as a chance to make her name by winning the biggest case this town had seen in decades—prosecuted this as murder one.

That case had been the first major crack in her belief in the tight relationship between law and justice. The law said this man was a murderer. Justice said he was a hero.

After that she began reading everything she could on that relationship: law and justice; justice and law. And she started asking questions: why, if white collar and especially corporate crime costs the public more than ten times as much as street crime, and kills far more people, do law enforcement agencies focus so much on street crime? And why, when white collar or corporate criminals are caught, do they so rarely go to jail, much less prison? And why are ecoterrorists threatened with literally more than a thousand years in prison for destroying property when tobacco company executives never stepped behind bars? Why, when law enforcement officers were called in to resolve strikes, do they always force strikers to terms, and never capitalists? Why do men who beat their wives or girlfriends to death receive average sentences of seven years, while those wives or girlfriends who fight back and kill their attackers receive average sentences of twenty years? And why is the agency spending so much time and money chasing this Malia Jennings woman when the man she murdered clearly killed far more—thousands more—than she did? So far as Jessica could tell, he'd never even received a visit from the IRS, much less the FBI. Bullets or cancer, dead is dead. How was Malia really different than that young man who killed the abuser? Both stopped someone who was harming their community.

She'd often wished she could have been a county sheriff on that young man's case. She would have been tempted to misplace evidence or break the evidence chain, somehow get the guy off. It might have wrecked her career, but better her career than his life.

But of course she hadn't been on the case, and course if she had been on that case, she never would have had the guts to act so decisively against the law—to be such a "bad girl," and in fact to go against her oath to uphold the law. But didn't she break that oath every day of the week by not going after corporate criminals? Oath-breaking or not, she knew she wouldn't have had the courage: she doesn't even have the courage to ask for a transfer away from this lousy section run by her lousy obnoxious sexist supervisor, Donald.

Larry Gordon doesn't want to die, but he's already dead. He knows that. Entombed in a metal coffin, he waits for the bullet he knows will come. He can't believe this is going to happen. He can't believe this is going to happen to him.

He can't move. He can't see. He can't hear over the engine's roar, the muffler's rumble, the tires' whine. He can barely breathe. Something covers his head, and he feels his hot breath come back to him, on his lips, his nostrils, his cheeks. He tastes it, warm, wet, filled with fear. Again and again he breathes the same air. But he is breathing. He isn't dead yet. He won't die. Not yet.

His hands are bound behind his back. He feels metal above, below, in front, behind. He's on his side. There's no room to extend his legs. But he can kick. He coils his legs and pounds them against the metal beyond his feet. A thud. He does it again. And again. Perhaps he can kick a hole.

Over the noise, he hears a voice from the front of the car, "Cut the shit or we waste you right here."

He isn't dead yet. Someone spoke. He doesn't want to die. He quits kicking.

He's in the trunk of a car. He feels every bounce. Every pothole bangs his head on the floor. He smells rubber from the spare tire, and dust, and old gas, faint, sweet, sickening. It makes him want to retch, but he knows if he does he will suffocate. He forces it down. He doesn't want to die.

Calm. Calm. He has to stay calm. He has to make himself calm. If he's going to live he has to think, he has to find an angle. He has to free his wrists. Then maybe he can open the latch and jump out. He finds the edge of the spare tire well with his fingers, and begins to scrape the tape that binds his wrists along the layered metal. The tape slides smoothly across the surface, and then snags as he finds a burr. He pushes hard, and feels his skin tear as it catches on the protruding metal. But he doesn't feel any loosening of the tape. Again and again he tries, until his muscles begin to cramp from the unfamiliar movement. His muscles spasm uncontrollably.

More skin tears. Still the tape remains tight.

Rubber, gas, dirt, fear. The smells swirl in his brain. He wants to cry. He wants to break down. But he can't do that. If he loses control he's dead. That he knows.

Okay, what else does he know? He knows he was taken from just outside his home. He knows he's going to die, and he knows the reason. It's because of one moment of stupidity. He knows if he could take back just that one moment, he wouldn't die. Driving home from work—an hour ago, a half hour, three hours, a lifetime—he'd seen a car parked blocking the gate that led to his driveway. Its hood was up. The thought occurred: why would someone break down here? But he didn't drive away. Instead he stopped behind them, got out of his car, stepped forward, and asked what was their problem. One of them, their leader—leader of what?—turned to him and said, calm, as though speaking of a faulty distributor, "You are." Another, who'd been leaning under the hood, stood straight, and Gordon had seen that instead of a wrench the man held a gun. A third had come up from behind and thrown something over Gordon's head. They put him in the trunk, and now he's going to die.

He has to know why. If he can reason his way through that, perhaps he can talk them out of it. Yes. They have no reason to kill him. He doesn't even know who they are. Perhaps they have the wrong man, and perhaps when they finally stop the car he can tell them that. Maybe then they'll release him. They have to. It's all a mistake. He has no enemies. How could he? He's never harmed anyone.

He knows that he hurts. His back hurts from where it hit the latch on the way into the trunk, his arms hurt from the cramping, his hands hurt where he scraped away the skin, his ribs hurt from rubbing against the spare tire, and his neck hurts from trying, mainly unsuccessfully, to keep his head from bouncing off the trunk's metal bed.

The car speeds on. Gordon searches for a way out. He will not be stupid twice. This time he'll be prepared. Again and again in his mind he replays that one moment of stopping his car: of seeing them, raising his eyebrows slightly in surprise, touching the brakes, coasting to a stop. Because of that—simply because of that—he's going to die. From now on he'll take care of himself. He wants another chance, a chance to choose life, to see their car and drive on by. He doesn't think he'll get it.

The car stops, and Larry Gordon expects someone to come and open the trunk. He expects to be carried away. But no one comes. Low voices from the front. Three of them. He can't make them out. But there are three. Then silence. Then he makes out a voice: "Showtime."

Now it will come. He hears and feels a door open, then shut. He waits. Nothing. He still waits. What are they doing? Now two voices from the front. The radio, loud for a moment, and then just as quickly silent.

Time passes, and still no one comes for him. If it weren't for the sporadic voices from the front, he would wonder if they were going to leave him in here all night. Then the car door opens and shuts again. Still no one comes for him. This time he hears the sound of someone's shoes scuffing on a hard surface, getting fainter as the person walks away.

Lying in the trunk, sweating, breath coming in foul-tasting catches, muscles cramping in his neck, arms, legs, deep aches in his ribs, Larry Gordon wishes he had more time. Not just time now, before he has to hear footfalls approach the back of the car, before he hears the metallic scrape of key on lock and the click of lock's release, before he feels the hood being removed from his head and finds himself staring at the face of this young man he has never seen before, and thinking, *This man's face, this asphalt, this car, the blue-black of this gun's barrel, these are the last things I'll ever see.* Even if he gets out of this, he still will want—still will need—more time. Because there's something he doesn't understand. Something. Time. That's what he needs.

Sitting at her desk, looking intently at this young man who's looking just as intently back at her, Malia feels her life of activism—the life she knows and enjoys—slipping away from her. She says, "I can't . . ." then stops, not knowing how to finish. She asks, "Why did you bring him *here?*"

"I thought you'd want to know—"

She interrupts, "—Is he dead?—"

"No, and—"

"What do you *want* from me?"

Dujuan says, simply, ingenuously, "We brought him here because we thought you'd know what he's guilty of. As much as anyone would."

"So?"

"So if we gonna have a trial we need to have somebody who knows what's what."

"I don't get it. You're gonna turn him over to the cops and then try to prosecute him?"

Dujuan makes a gesture with his face, a slight lifting of his chin as though letting her in on a private joke. He says, eyes smiling, "You bein stupid again."

Malia says, "I was gonna say, they'll never pros—" She stops a long moment, then says, "What are you telling me?"

Dujuan says, "I'll let him tell you." He calls out Simon's name. Simon, who had approached to outside her door without Malia hearing, steps inside. Dujuan gestures again with his head, this time jerking it sharply in the direction of the parking lot. Malia follows the motion, as if by looking closely enough she can see through the walls. Simon nods and steps back out.

Malia puts her head in her hands. She says, "You can't do this."

Dujuan responds, "My sister's dead. You said Vexcorp did it. Convince me."

Malia looks back up to him and slowly shakes her head. She says, "I need time to think about this."

She wants to work her way intellectually through the problem she faces. But she can't even define it. Her brain refuses to function. She sits, frozen. Dujuan's eyes smile again. She doesn't understand. His smile, and her not understanding his smile, bothers her. She thinks he might be laughing at her, then decides he's not. But he does seem to be enjoying himself.

He makes that same small gesture with his chin, and says, "Time's up."

She hears someone's voice, her own, say, "What if I refuse?"

He shrugs. "We walk."

"And if I call the cops?"

The smile reaches his mouth. He winks, then says, "We run."

She says, "Shit."

"But you ain't gonna do that," he says.

"I'm not?" Still confused.

Dujuan says, "You want this as bad as me."

Dear Anthony,

I'm sorry I broke down in our last conversation. You're right. Of course you're right. It would be far too dangerous for me to come see you. But the fact that it's too dangerous—and thank you for specifying that your fear is far more for me than for you—doesn't mean I don't want to.

Thank you for saying that you want to see me, too. And thank you even more for saying that you love me. That means so much to me.

I want you not just because I'm lonely, and not just because my life has been hard these past few years. I want you because of our conversations, both years ago and far more importantly now. I want you because of you, and because of us.

But I understand your point. Believe me, I understand it. I won't come to see you.

I love you,

Malia

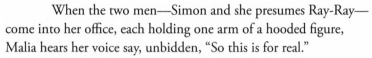

When the two men—Simon and she presumes Ray-Ray—come into her office, each holding one arm of a hooded figure, Malia hears her voice say, unbidden, "So this is for real."

Dujuan frowns.

Malia says, "I thought . . ." She tries to make her mind work. "The Feds . . ."

Ray-Ray looks alarmed, until Dujuan catches Ray-Ray's eye and shakes his head.

Malia's thoughts continue unsteady. "Maybe they . . ."

Silence for a moment before Dujuan understands. He laughs and says, "You thought the Feds were tryin to fuck you up? Why would they do that to *you?*"

Simon laughs now, and Ray-Ray, too.

Malia doesn't laugh. She realizes on some level she had been hoping, farcically, that this was a setup. She knows that Fed agents routinely instigate illegal activities to entrap activists. That would have made her response simple: she would just have told Dujuan—the Fed *provocateur*—to go to hell, and the incident would have had a happy ending. The feds would have been happy because they almost infiltrated CAT; Larry Gordon because he kept making money; Malia because her work was dangerous enough to attract the FBI's attention; Dennis because this proved the need to stay legal. But Malia knows that Fed entrapment can't extend to kidnapping.

She stares at the figure in front of her. Over his head is a dark blue sweatshirt, arms tied loosely around his neck. A mass of duct tape closes off the neck hole and also attaches the body of the sweatshirt to the man's clothing. His hands are taped behind his back.

Simon sees Malia stare at the mass of tape—excessive and messy like a little boy's Christmas wrapping—and says, sheepishly, "We never done this before."

Malia shrugs. Ray-Ray and Simon walk the figure to the chair facing Malia's desk and sit him down. Ray-Ray begins to untie the knotted arms of the sweatshirt and to remove the tape attached to Gordon's shirt.

Malia starts to her feet, saying, "Wait! He'll see us."

Now Dujuan shrugs. "He's already seen me."

"But he hasn't seen *me.*"

Dujuan thinks a moment before reaching to pull the sweatshirt off Gordon's head. He says to Malia, "Welcome to the club."

Malia stares at Larry Gordon. He's of medium height and has a bit of a paunch. His hair is graying and very short. His eyes are a striking blue. He's scared, and breathing quickly. She's seen his picture before, yet now his normally pale complexion is pallid with fright. He sits on the edge of the chair. He blinks his eyes in the light, says, "My hands . . ."

Dujuan nods and Ray-Ray cuts the tape binding his arms. Ray-Ray says, "Put your hands—"

Gordon puts his hands on the arms of the chair.

Ray-Ray says, "Good boy," and tapes his arms in place.

Gordon continues to blink, though less frequently now, and to breathe heavily. Malia watches him carefully. Sensing her stare, Gordon brings his eyes to hers. He examines her closely and a flash of recognition crosses his face. He nods. His breathing slows. He begins to smile. Malia knows from this smile that he thinks her presence will guarantee his safety. Malia doesn't like how that makes her feel.

Enunciating clearly, he says, "I *know* you. You are Malia Louise Jennings, the woman from the fundraiser, that little dog that has been yapping at my heels all these years." After a pause, he continues, "If you wanted an appointment, you should have called my secretary." Then he's silent as he surveys the room. When his eyes land on the posters on the wall, he says, "Che Guevara? This is a very bad movie indeed." He looks at Malia. "What is this, the latest sort of sit-in? Instead of occupying my office you've brought me to occupy yours? Good media trick . . . but you forgot the cameras."

No one says anything. Malia hopes Dujuan isn't expecting her to make the next move, because she doesn't know what to do. But Dujuan steps close to Gordon and hunkers down. Neither speaks.

Finally, Gordon says, "Enough of your game. What do you want?"

Dujuan stares deeply into Gordon's eyes, then whispers, "Justice."

"What?"

At last Malia speaks, "He said he wants justice."

Gordon shakes his head. "I have no idea what you're talking about."

Malia thinks, *Of course you don't.*

Gordon says, "Do you know how foolish it is to talk about justice when you've got a gun on the table?"

Dujuan speaks, still quietly, still inches from Gordon's face, "That's the only way you'll talk. About my sister."

Gordon looks honestly taken aback.

Still quietly, "You killed my sister."

"I've never killed anyone."

Silence, before Dujuan says, "Shameka Browning."

Gordon's face clears. "I hate to break the news, but you've kidnapped the wrong man."

Malia says, "You poisoned her."

"You're mistaken."

"No, he's not. Vexcorp's effluents killed his sister. She died of cancer."

"So *that's* what this is about." Gordon shakes his head, and comments to Malia, "You finally found someone who believes you."

Dujuan responds quickly, "She finally found someone who don't need Vexcorp for a paycheck."

Gordon, dismissively, almost airily, says, "Oh, did *she* pay you? I don't know what she—"

Malia speaks over him, "And his father."

Gordon forces his voice back over hers, "—has against us. Against the whole community."

Simon breaks in now, as well, "My aunt, too. And Ray-Ray's cousin."

Gordon sighs, then says, "Release me."

No one moves.

"Now," Gordon says. It's clear he's used to being obeyed.

Malia says, "I don't think you understand your predicament."

"I understand I've been kidnapped by Che Guevara and her three stooges . . ."

Ray-Ray steps up close behind Gordon and takes the man's chin in his hand. He jerks Gordon's head back and to the side, says, "Big words for such a little man."

Gordon is nonplussed. "You think because I'm tied up you're more powerful than me?"

Malia is confused. They're off track. She's not sure she wants them to stay on track, but she does sense that this sort of male jousting to see who's more powerful at this moment is especially pointless. She says, "Mr. Gordon . . ."

Gordon asks Ray-Ray, "How do you think I got where I am?"

Simon interjects, "Which do you mean, killing kids to make a buck, or tied up like a fuckin turkey?"

Malia tries again. "Mr. Gordon . . ."

Gordon continues talking to Ray-Ray, "I lunch with Senators, with the President, and the way I got here—"

Simon again, "—Was by inheritin a shitload of money—"

"—Was through hard work—"

"—Don't forget the killin—"

"—Work. Something none of you are familiar with."

Malia takes advantage of the short silence to say, "Mr. Gordon, you are here so you can be tried for murder."

Gordon struggles against the tape. He gets nowhere. He looks around the room, and then at Malia. "Murder? Whose murder?"

"His sister's."

No response.

She continues, "His twelve-year-old sister. His little sister. His baby sister."

Gordon looks at Dujuan, then says sincerely, "You think I killed your sister."

Dujuan responds, "What? You don't hear so well?"

No one speaks for a long moment before Gordon says, "You really think I killed your sister."

Still no one speaks.

Gordon continues, "You're all crazy."

More silence.

Gordon says, "I don't believe this."

Without hesitation, Dujuan answers, "Start believing it."

Once again, Jessica enters the Donald's office. She sits. She says, "We have a problem."

Donald looks at her, raises his eyebrows.

She says, "Anthony convinced Malia not to come see him. He says it's too dangerous."

"Fuck!" the man says.

The woman doesn't say anything.

"I'm tired of chasing that fucking bitch." He pauses, says to Jessica, "Nothing personal."

Jessica still doesn't say anything.

"Let me think," Donald says. "I'm sure I'll figure out some way to reel her in."

Dennis stands, takes a step, sways slightly as he hears the loud whirring of birds' wings in his head, then takes another step.

He's already paid his tab—after counting the money three times and still not getting it right—and it's time to go. He hasn't found anyone to go home with him, but he hasn't really looked. Had he looked, he was sure he would have found. And had he found, he would already have been home. But he's not at home, which means he must not have looked. QED. Simple as that. He can't go home anyway. He has to see Malia.

He takes another step, and wants to sit down. He wants to go to sleep, but can't, for he has miles to go. Three of them, in fact, or 3.4 according to his odometer. That's how far it is from The Marshlands to the Council. And he has to get there before Malia leaves. Maybe if he gets there before she leaves he can sit next to her, talk to her, hold her hand. Maybe they could . . . But even in his foggy state he knows those days are long over.

He wants to order another beer. He wants to go home and get some rest. He wants to go to the office and have Malia tell him that everything is going to be all right. He wants her to rock him to sleep.

He looks around the room and realizes he is surrounded by ghosts. Not just the other people, who like him, are pale, insubstantial shadows of who they really are, but also the tables, chairs, the recycled rubber floormats. The building itself. They're all specters, fleeting, unreal. The same is true of the sidewalk outside. The street. The Interstate. The concrete bridge that runs the length of the city.

He sees it now: the whole town is a phantom on the landscape. Beneath the pavement, grass. Beneath the buildings, hidden spaces and tunnels of rats and frogs and earthworms and spiders. All waiting for the day when the buildings collapse and the pavement cracks. Waiting.

Then he remembers the river. Dead. Fuck it all. The fucking rats probably have tumors on their tumors, and when the buildings collapse there will be nothing beneath but bones and fur.

And fuck it all even more, he realizes he's thinking like Malia. He hates that, and feels once again sorry for her, if this is the awareness—and he knows it is—she carries with her wherever she goes, like a coal that burns until it makes a hole right through you, yet never consumes itself and never goes away. He doesn't want to carry this awareness. Just right now he is too drunk to maintain his defenses, but not drunk enough to stop thinking. He needs another beer.

He'll go to the office in a while. Not right now. He signals the server, the most beautiful waitress in the world, and when she comes he asks for another Hope Street Bitter, and another order of fries.

Malia looks at Gordon, who looks at Dujuan.

Gordon is puzzled. He asks, not defiantly, but almost as though he's nothing more than curious, "What makes you think you have the right to judge me?"

Dujuan looks around conspiratorially, then leans close, as though sharing a secret. He says, "We don't got a lotta rights in this great fuckin country, but this is a right we're takin right now." He looks toward Simon and Ray-Ray, and says, "Right?"

Simon says, "Absofuckinglutely right."

Ray-Ray nods and says, "Right, Dujuan."

Turning back to Gordon, Dujuan says, "I guess we got the right. Three of them in fact."

Gordon responds, "If you're so sure I killed your sister, take me to court."

Dujuan picks a solid pencil holder off the desk, raps it twice on the wooden surface. He says, "Court's in session."

"You can't put me on trial."

"You gettin more than my sister ever got. At least you get to talk in your own defense."

"This is ridiculous. You can't kidnap somebody, stand over him with a gun, and pretend it's going to be a fair trial."

"Cops kidnap us with guns all the time. Nobody ever says nothin then." Dujuan pauses, then continues, "Besides, this gonna be the fairest trial you ever seen." He waits for Gordon to say something, and when it becomes evident Gordon doesn't understand, Dujuan explains, "Yo corporate lawyer friends can't protect you this time."

Silence, until Gordon says, still confused, "I started work as a corporate lawyer."

"Fuck," Dujuan responds, "Another charge for the prosecution."

Gordon finally has enough. He says, "Look. If you're going to demand ransom, just do it. Make the call. Disguise your voice. Do whatever it is you people do. I'm sure Vexcorp will pay."

Quickly, Dujuan says, "Fine. You wanna buy your way out? How much is yo life worth?"

Malia flinches. Ever since Dujuan arrived she's found herself having nearly as much difficulty as Gordon comprehending what's happening. For great long stretches she hears her voice responding to Dujuan or Gordon, but at no time does she feel herself an active agent. She thinks she now understands what it must feel like to be swept away by a flood, struggling hard to keep from drowning amidst all the fast movement, unable to find anything solid to grasp, no footholds of previous experience for purchase. She swims, seeing yet not seeing what passes before her, hearing acutely everything that is said yet not hearing any of it over the tumult. Every so often a sentence, a phrase, snatches at her, and suddenly for a moment she sees clearly what's unfolding in front of her, and sees clearly how the extent of her participation will change her own life, and then she grows afraid and tries to push herself away as though the mere act of feeling trepidation will lessen her involvement, and ultimately her penalty. She does not precisely want the events to stop. For she knows deep down that Dujuan is right: this is what she wants. This is part of what she has wanted for so very long. But she knows also that she does not want to be involved. Let someone else do it. Let someone else take the fall. Dennis, too, was right when he said to her that fear is the belief she has something left to lose. She thinks of her niece, of her mother and father, of the farm, and of the dailiness of her own work at the Council, and she is afraid. She has far too much to lose. Malia hears her voice ask, "What do you mean, what's his life worth?"

Dujuan says, "What do you think? We gonna sentence him to Club Fed with the other bigshot criminals, let him work on his tennis game?"

Simon pipes in, "Improve his tan."

Ray-Ray says, "Take up a hobby." He pauses, then continues, speaking directly to Malia, "You think this is some kinda joke?"

There's a strange silence before Malia hears her voice again, distant, as through water. She is at the bottom of the flood. "You're going to kill him."

Another silence, except for the rushing in her ears.

Gordon breaks the silence. "Kill me. Kill me? All right. Fine. Go. Go . . . go ahead. There's the gun. What are you waiting for? Just blow my brains out, if that's what it takes to be a man, to avenge the dead. Go ahead and hold your little court, but let's be clear about what this is: murder."

From somewhere deep underwater Malia listens to the conversation. She hears Simon say to Ray-Ray, "You were right. We should have just waxed his ass."

Gordon looks at Simon defiantly. "You don't like the message, so you're going to kill the messenger."

Dujuan: "No, we don't like the decision, so we gonna kill the decision-maker."

Gordon: "Typical brutish reaction."

Dujuan says, slowly, "Fine, motherfucka. Make a better decision. Refine me."

Malia tries to swim to the surface. Her voice: "I don't . . ."

Everyone ignores her. Gordon says, "Listen. I'm not going to sit here and explain the benefits . . . Vexcorp's the only good thing that's happened to this slum in the last fifty years. And you want to destroy it."

From a corner of the room Malia sees herself begin to stand, then sit back down. She says, "Something's not right here."

They continue to ignore her. Dujuan says to Gordon,

"Maybe so. From yo side it is the best thing that's ever happened, cause it's making you rich and killin us off."

Gordon responds, "You don't know what you're talking about."

"I'm talkin bout poison."

"Oh. Are you a toxicologist?"

"A toxifuckamacallit?"

Gordon grunts.

Dujuan leans close, and says, "You don't have to be a gynecologist to know you gettin fucked up the ass."

Gordon sneers. "The word's proctologist. If you're going to—"

Malia turns to Dujuan, "I don't know if this is right."

Dujuan stares at her, then stalks to one of the posters on the wall and points. "You talked about this guy. Who is he?"

"Che Guevara. He led revolutions across South America."

"What happened to him?"

"He was murdered by the Bolivian military."

"And he fought for poor people?"

"Yes."

Dujuan rips down the poster. "Then don't fuckin put his picture on the wall if he don't mean nothin to you." He hesitates before continuing, "You started this whole thing, talkin about us doin the same as him, and now you ain't got the balls . . . I don't know who's more pathetic, this fuckin killer or you. You got a better idea than what we doin? Has yo precious little job here done jack for us all these years?"

Malia can't speak.

Dujuan asks again, spearing the air with his finger, "Has it?"

More silence. Malia hates herself, hates the position she's in. Most of all she hates Dujuan for putting her in it.

Dujuan continues, pointing first to Malia and then to Gordon, "You guys, you two fuckin sides of the same coin. You make me sick. You wanna stop these motherfuckers but you want us to do the killin, and these motherfuckers say they bring good things to life, but it's always us doin the dyin. You sit there all full of care and concern when it comes to pointin the gun at this guy, but you had no problem at all pointin it at me when I came in." He moves around her desk next to her, and says, "Why don't you grow a fuckin backbone and pick a side?"

She doesn't say anything.

Dujuan says to Ray-Ray and Simon, "Let's take this fucker out and dump him."

Gordon says, "So this 'trial' crap is all a charade."

Dujuan walks back around the desk to Gordon and snaps his head up. "You ain't worth a fuckin bullet. You two can just keep playin yo little bullshit games while real people keep dyin." To Ray-Ray and Simon he says, "Let's go."

Malia hears her voice say, "Wait."

Dujuan turns to face her. She says nothing. She can neither move nor speak.

Dujuan says to her, "You know what I just realized? This ain't real to you. You think this is a big fuckin computer game. Somebody dies and you just restart the fuckin game and you get another person. You don't feel pain. You don't feel loss. What do you care? It's just a fuckin game." He pauses, then points at her. "Well, I got news for you. People feel pain, and then they die. I saw my sister go through pain, and then I saw her die. *My* sister. It ain't yo family dying. If it was, if you knew anything about pain, you would know what to do right now."

At last Malia finds strength. "My mother has cancer."

"An what the fuck you goin do about it?"

"Don't talk to me that way."

"That's weak. You can do better than that."

"You say I don't know anything about pain," she says. "But I know what it's like to be a woman. And I know what it's like to be beaten. By you."

He turns toward the door. Malia says, "Wait."

Silence in the room as once again he turns to face her.

Malia says, slowly, "I do want things to change."

No one says a word.

She continues, still slowly, "I would do anything, give up my life to stop the poison. But I have a question for you."

Dujuan doesn't help her out.

Malia gestures vaguely at the gun on the table, and asks, "Do you really believe this will help?"

More silence. It hurts Malia's ears.

Finally, Dujuan says, "It's a start."

Jessica knows this is terrible. Donald had told Jessica his plan, and it's absolutely terrible. It's illegal, unethical, and unnecessarily combative. In other words, pure Donald.

And Jessica thinks it won't work. If she were allowed to give input, which she now knows will never happen with Donald, and if she were to want to solve this case—she's no longer sure she does—she would handle it entirely differently.

Donald and Jessica go to the house that Anthony once shared with Malia. They know already from surveillance photos that there's only one road into the property. On the other side is a forest. They get out of their rented car. Two old dogs come to greet them. The agents knock on the door.

Anthony answers.

The man says, "My name is Donald Spalding, and this is Jessica Keller."

Anthony responds quickly, "I'm not interested in accepting Jesus Christ as my personal savior."

"We're not Jehovah's Witnesses. We're federal agents."

"I'm even less interested in being saved by you."

"The question isn't whether you're interested in talking to us. It's whether we're interested in talking to you. And the answer is yes."

Jessica can tell how much Donald is enjoying this. She would say loving this, but she doesn't think he loves anything. She also knows he has no idea how much she hates it. He makes her embarrassed to be in the Bureau.

"I've got nothing to say to you. Please leave my property."

Donald smiles through thin lips, says, "Or what? You'll call the cops? You're laboring under the delusion that your opinion matters. It doesn't. We know you've been talking with Malia Jennings. And now you're going to talk to us."

"No."

Donald turns to Jessica, says, "'No,' the man says. That's a nice joke, isn't it?"

part five

She wants more than anything to say, "No, Donald, he's well within his rights not to talk to you. He asked you to leave his property, and it is our obligation to do so. You're shredding the constitution you're supposed to protect. And you're a fool if you think this is going to succeed. He'll never cooperate with you now. If I were in charge I could soft-talk him into working with us, but that's just not your way, is it?" She says none of this.

Donald steps toward the front door, says, "Aren't you going to ask us in?"

Larry Gordon looks at the tape that binds his wrists to the arms of the chair, and he feels alive. Every muscle and every nerve sings. This is what life is really about.

It all comes down to power, Gordon thinks. Who has it, who fears it, who is able to grasp it, take it in hand, wield it, and finally, who deserves it. In the end, nothing else matters. Except winning, which is nothing more than a measure of one's power anyway. And Gordon knows he's going to win.

It hadn't taken him long to dismiss Ray-Ray and Simon; in fact he'd done so almost immediately. For all Ray-Ray's talk, Gordon knows he's essentially without power, and so is irrelevant to the night's outcome. Simon even moreso. Gordon knows he can deal with these two at a later date, at his convenience.

Malia is only a bit more complicated. She thinks she has power, but that power is circumscribed by scruple. Her problem, simply put, is her reliance on what she considers a moral structure. Larry Gordon positively cannot die tonight, because she positively cannot kill him. She doesn't see that morality is more complex than that, and considerably more pliable. An action that may be moral in one circumstance may be immoral in another, and in a third may be simply stupid. Anyone who doesn't know that, he thinks, knows nothing of power, and even less of morals.

Dujuan is the most difficult case, but even he is a child. The only thing that scares Gordon about Dujuan is his bestial nature, his animal unpredictability. Gordon feels that the best approach will be to keep Dujuan just off-balance enough to not allow him to take the offensive, but not so near to toppling that he does something rash, something they'll all regret. Even more important is to keep him listening to Malia. Gordon knows he'll have to play them off each other, and whenever Dujuan becomes too imbalanced, use Malia to pull him back to stability.

All this Larry Gordon surmises sitting in the chair, listening to Dujuan and Malia. All this he believes to be true. He honestly believes he feels no fear, nor confusion, that all is in control. His control.

Anthony leaves his home at two in the morning. He drives. He drives in large multi-block loops, he drives in straight lines, he suddenly turns left or suddenly turns right. At last he is convinced that no one is following him.

He continues to drive. At last he parks a couple of miles from a friend's house, to cover the possibility of a tracking device having been attached to his car. He walks the rest of the way. He pushes her doorbell. He pushes it again. She finally answers. She lets him in.

He says, "Charlotte Jane, I'm in trouble."

"I know," she says.

"How?"

"You haven't used my middle name since the night your dad died."

They sit on her couch. He says, "I need your help. Malia contacted me."

"Malia," she says. "It's been so long."

"But that's not the problem."

"Of course not."

"The feds came by last week. They know—"

"How?" she asks.

"The phone."

She doesn't say anything.

His throat is tight. He forces a cough so she won't know how close he is to sobbing. He says, "They told me that if I don't set her up, they'll throw me in prison."

"For what? What have you possibly done?"

"You know that doesn't matter. You know how they work."

"What are you going to do?"

"I don't know what to do. I don't see what my options are. That's why I came to you."

A few minutes pass, and Malia understands the direction her life has to take, if anything she has ever done is to mean anything. She says to Gordon, "I believe we can take it for granted that you're guilty—"

Gordon sits upright, for the first time surprised by her.

She continues, "—And the only question—"

Dujuan interjects, "—Kill him—"

Malia finishes, "—is what to do with you."

Gordon shakes his head. "I'm not guilty."

Malia rolls her eyes. "Oh, please."

"This girl, I don't even know who you're talking about."

No one speaks until Malia says, somewhat patronizingly, "It's very simple. Does Vexcorp refine and also release toxic chemicals?"

Gordon takes a deep breath, and when he speaks Malia notices he matches her patronizing tone. "We refine bulk chemicals, which if used properly are crucial to many modern industrial processes—"

Malia interrupts, "We."

"Listen. Do you eat food? Live in a house? Then you need us. Pesticides, formaldehyde for plywood, polypropylene for clothes. We make life bearable. Livable. This city couldn't exist without us."

She says again. "We. So you identify yourself with Vexcorp?"

"I'm telling you Vexcorp is important not only to this community but to the economy." He pauses. "And, no, I'm not the company. I own stock—"

"—4 billion dollars worth—" Malia says.

"Jesus," Ray-Ray says, "We *should* call in a ransom."

Gordon says, "The company is democratically run, one vote per stock share to elect directors, who vote on all major issues."

"That's interesting," Malia responds. "Have you ever seen a proxy vote that went against the directors' recommendations?"

"Not many, no."

"Not many as in zero?"

"I'd have to check records . . ."

"And would it be fair to say you greatly benefit from the decisions of these directors, of which you're one?"

"That's not a fair question. Decisions are made in accordance with the letter and intent of the law of the land."

"No," Malia says. "The law of the government."

"What?"

Malia repeats, "*The government.* Not the land, not the people. I don't remember voting for a law saying you could pollute." She turns to Dujuan. "Did you vote on it?" Then back to Gordon. "So who made the decision? Why'd you put a factory here?"

"As in . . . ?"

Dujuan interrupts, "Why don't you poison yo own backyard?

"I don't poison anyone. If used and disposed of properly—"

Dujuan explodes, "Then why the fuck don't you live next door to me? How come you don't live on 144th Street?"

Gordon pauses a moment before he says, "Because I've got money."

"No shit."

Gordon says quietly, reasonably, "If you had money you'd move out of this dump, too."

Gordon wins that round.

✦

Barbara stands and walks to the picture window in the downstairs living room of her home. She's been sitting on the sofa in front of the television, watching the old black-and-white movie *Gaslight*. She prefers this production—the 1944 version with Charles Boyer and Ingrid Bergman—over the earlier film of the same name, primarily on the strength of Bergman's performance. Normally she enjoys watching Bergman's portrayal of a woman being systematically driven mad—especially because she knows the ending is happy—but tonight the film just makes her edgy.

She doesn't know where her husband is. She can't remember a time in their marriage when he has been absent so late without calling to let her know why. At the beginning she loved his solidity, his consistency, but she doesn't anymore. She hates it all. She pictures cement coagulating into a rigid block with her in the center. She can't breathe. She thinks about the pedestal that he has put her on ever since he first met her. For a time she liked her position, and had been flattered to be held up for acclaim, but she soon realized the pillar was too tall, the sides too steep, and she couldn't get down.

She stares at her reflection in the picture window, the hollows of her eyes deep and ghostly, the edges of her face blurred by the way the light reflects off the double-glazing. There are shadows on her right side, away from the light, dark beside and beneath her nose, and in the space between her cheek and her hair. She doesn't move, but stares at the face in front of her.

Finally she crosses to the switch and turns off the light, then walks to the couch and hits the remote. The television screen goes blank. Back by the window she turns on the light outside, sees the brick of the porch, and beyond that the black asphalt of the driveway forming a darker U against the dark night, and then beyond that the green of the grass turning black as the light disperses. She stays there long enough that moths begin beating themselves against the porch light. She sees one the size of a hummingbird.

When she was young she knew its name. She doesn't anymore. She looks far down the driveway, to where the gravel path turns and disappears into trees near the street, but she doesn't see a pair of headlamps announce her husband's return.

She isn't sure what she should do. She already tried his cellphone, and got no answer. Should she call the police? For what? Call her mother? Same question. What would she report?

She wanders back to the sofa, and this time does not turn on the television. She thinks instead about business trips her husband has taken over the years, and she remembers nights alone in their bed, hoping he wouldn't call, that instead she would pick up the phone and it would be someone from the airlines, or from the company, or police, someone telling her there had been some sort of an accident, and he wouldn't be coming home. But instead the phone would ring, she would pick it up, and she would hear his voice.

Tonight, though, the phone doesn't ring, and she is scared. She begins to cry.

Malia asks, "Why did you put the refinery here?"

"Tax breaks. Cheap land from the city. Regulatory relief—"

"—meaning?"

"Meaning we don't have to meet the same standards as factories elsewhere."

"What do you mean by standards? Workers' wages? Parking lot size? Daycare?"

Gordon knows where she's going: "Why don't you get to the real question?"

"The real question. You're in this room because your factory kills people."

He shakes his head emphatically, starts to say, "You can't pr—"

Malia doesn't let him finish: "Does the factory pollute?"

Gordon is silent for a moment before he says,

"Contamination here is already high. We do nothing different than anybody else."

"So you admit—"

"—I admit nothing—"

"—the factory emits carcinogens."

"Never," Gordon says. He's like a rock. "Not shown."

Dujuan asks, "Where'd my sister get cancer, then?"

Gordon looks him over carefully, sniffs once, then says, "You smell like you smoke. And does your family eat fried foods and other junk? Take drugs? You also smell of marijuana." He pauses, then says, looking first at Dujuan and then at the other two men, "You mentioned your father, and some of your relatives." He looks back to Dujuan, then says, firmly yet gently, as though softly reprimanding one of his own children, "Don't try to blame your family's lifestyle on me."

After a moment of confused silence, Dujuan looks to Malia and starts to ask, "Is he—"

Gordon continues, "—Tragic, but not criminal, and nothing to do with—"

Dujuan looks back at Gordon, "You sayin—"

Gordon still talks, "—my company whatsoever—"

Dujuan finishes his sentence, "—my own family killed my sister."

Gordon shakes his head, and says, still softly, "No, no, no, no. Not in—"

Dujuan picks up the gun on Malia's desk. "Court's over. He's done."

Were Gordon not strapped to the chair he would have leapt to his feet. Dujuan holds his gun, small and shiny in his hand.

Gordon says, quickly, quietly, "I appreciate your pain. I . . . I can understand the questions you've asked yourself over and over: 'What could I have done differently? Could I have caught it sooner, could I have taken her to a different hospital?'"

Dujuan blinks slowly, noncommittal.

Gordon continues, quietly "I didn't do it, son. Listen to

me. She's wrong. I'd be happy to show you reams of studies showing minor chemical releases from the plant are well under all safety standards. We've done so many risk analyses you wouldn't believe it—"

For all Dujuan's talk, it's clear he doesn't want to kill. It's just as clear that Gordon perceives this wavering, and takes heart. Malia begins to look through the Vexcorp file on the corner of her desk. She says, "Analyses?"

Gordon continues, "Any increase might be on the order of one or two per hundred thousand, which is nothing like the epidemic you're describing."

Still searching, Malia asks, "Mr. Gordon, do you fish?"

"—Are you sure it was even cancer? . . . What? Do I fish? Occasionally. Why?"

She asks, "Do you fish this river?"

"My office is uptown," he says. "I rarely come down here."

"Signs warn people to eat no more than one fish per year, and not to swim where more than one out of four fish have open sores." She continues to search through the file.

"Regulatory excess," Gordon responds. "Come to think of it, I have eaten fish from the river."

Simon remarks, "Then you're dumber'n you look . . ."

"Nonsense," Gordon rebuts, "The only way those fish could poison you is if you eat thousands, and even then you'd have to eat the bones. We have studies, done by in-house scientists—"

Malia finds the paper she was looking for. She casually holds it in front of him and says, "Speaking of studies, do you recognize this?"

"I can't . . . the light . . ."

"Take your time."

"What?"

"Your handwriting? Your signature?"

"This is all out of context—"

"Tell me again," Malia says, "that your factory doesn't pollute." She turns to Dujuan and says, "These are notes written by Larry Gordon during a confidential board meeting six years ago." She begins to read, haltingly because the handwriting is a fast scrawl, "Soils tests: Toxic at six miles. Release test results? Board vote: twelve to zero against. Water: toxic at two miles. Release test results? Board vote: twelve to zero against. Increase pollution abatement: cost fifty-five million. Board vote: twelve to zero against. Purchase adjacent lands: cost one hundred and twenty-five million. Board vote: unanimous against. Costs of continuing operations: see El Paso study for similar lawsuits: five to ten thousand per kid—"

Dujuan says, "Wait—"

Malia gestures gently for him to be quiet, "Board vote: twelve to zero for. Organize defensive legal posture. Board vote: twelve to zero for. Fund scientists for defensive scientific posture. Board vote: twelve to zero for. Call Cash tomorrow: he'll work Senate. Call Chris at paper to get favorable editorials. All notes to be shredded within forty-eight hours."

No one speaks for a few moments. Finally Simon breaks the silence. "They actually say shit like that?"

Gordon begins, "I—"

Dujuan cuts him off, "Shut up." Dujuan squats in front of Gordon, and studies him intently. He says, "And you've got the nerve to tell me *I* should be locked up."

Gordon begins, "D—"

Dujuan stops him again, "—Don't."

At last, Gordon says, "Do you want money?"

Dujuan cocks the gun. "No."

Gordon meets his stare, and says, "You have proven no connection between that piece of paper and the death of your sister."

Dujuan responds, "I'm tired of people takin me for stupid. Everybody sees the connection."

"But not to *her* cancer."

Dujuan says, "Anybody's. Take your pick."

He puts his hand on Gordon's shoulder, pushes him back in the chair. With his other hand he places the gun against

Gordon's belly. He says, "This will be for my father."

He moves the gun to touch over Gordon's heart, and says, "This will be for my sister."

He puts the gun to Gordon's head, "But this one I'll enjoy the most because it will be all for me."

At last Gordon panics. For the first time he understands that he might actually die. He says, quickly, his mind and his tongue stumbling over words, "Wait. Listen. That was one meeting. Ideas in a meeting. Just notes. It means nothing. We didn't do any of it. I regret we even mentioned it."

He hears Malia say, "This happens every day. The only thing you regret is that you left notes, and that your secretary had enough of a conscience to mail us a copy."

June Karr. The secretary he'd fired. But they have it all wrong.

Dujuan says to Malia, "Those notes are six years old? Where the hell were the feds? You *did* tell them."

"Of course."

"And?"

"You expect the feds to protect you? You expect them to punish the rich for killing the poor? Now you're the one being stupid, Dujuan. Cash did the job right. No jail term, no fine. No indictment. No arrest. No nothing. Legislation exempting Vexcorp from liability. Business as usual."

Gordon says, "But we didn't do anything . . ."

Dujuan releases his hold on Gordon and steps toward Malia. "Lemme see that."

She hands him the page. He looks it over and hands it to Simon, who hands it to Ray-Ray. When Ray-Ray finishes he puts it on the desk.

Dujuan says to Gordon, "If you've got anything to say, say it now."

"It's not my fault."

Dujuan looks at Malia and asks, "What do they call that?"

"I believe the technical term is denial."

Gordon doesn't know what they're talking about. He's going to die for nothing.

"You don't understand. Malia, make them stop! I'll tell you how it is. A man in my position, the position I'm in, I'm a prisoner. You don't have choices. You have to go along with the system. If you're good, it rewards you. If not, you get punished. You laugh—"

Simon asks, "Who's laughing?"

"—but that's the way it is—"

Simon continues, "Ain't nobody laughing here, mofo."

Gordon speaks as quickly as possible, saying anything to forestall death, "Don't you see? I could have been jailed if I didn't maximize profits. Tell him, Malia, tell him! And Dujuan, it's the whole thing, see. It's not me. Why do you think corporations exist? The purpose of a corporation is to make money. That's all it can do. If it can make money poisoning kids, poisoning rivers, it is required by law to do so. Don't you see? I don't matter. I'm just a name. I'm nothing. Ask her. Go on, ask her! I'm right, aren't I?"

Malia shrugs and says, "He's right, it's structural."

"That's it!" Gordon sees she understands. Now she'll help him make these others understand. He says, "So it won't do any good to kill me, see. I'm not responsible."

Malia shrugs again and says, "No more than Adolph Eichmann."

Gordon pauses a moment. He thinks, *No, she doesn't understand. She's insane. They're all insane.* He says, to Dujuan, "It's all competition. Survival of the fittest. If Vexcorp doesn't keep costs down, if we spend profits to control pollution, somebody else eats us up, like we're a tiny little fish."

Dujuan asks, "Who makes the structure? Who gains? Who pays? Didn't you ever think that you could change the structure?"

"But that's just it." Now Dujuan and Gordon are talking. Man to man. Things are going to work out. Gordon will make them work out, no matter what it takes. He says, "This is how things work, out in the real world. It's economics. It's politics. It's the whole ball of wax. That's what it's all about. I just go along, one little fish floating in the current."

Gordon stares hard into Dujuan's eyes and suddenly realizes Dujuan hasn't been moved by anything he's said. Gordon feels his eyelids close almost on their own, and feels his chin fall to his chest, as though he's fainted. He's silent for a long moment, then suddenly brings his head up and says, fiercely, "What are you going to do, kill all of us? There were twelve members on that board. And then what? Are you going to go company to company?"

Dujuan reaches into his shirt pocket for a piece of paper. He says, "Names and addresses."

Gordon says, "That's mass murder."

Dujuan shakes his head. "Payback."

"And I'm the first casualty."

"Yeah, you number one," Dujuan responds. "You'd like that, wouldn't you? You could be some kinda martyr. But you ain't even the first. My sister. My dad. All the rest. You started it, but you call it business." Dujuan pauses a moment, then continues, "If you don't do it somebody else will. What kinda crackbrain copout is that? I couldn't use that excuse on my mom when I was a kid, why should I let you use it now?"

Gordon realizes what his mistake had been. How could he possibly have expected this thug to understand economics, the real world? Dujuan is as stupid as Malia, and as insane. They're out of touch with reality, driven mad by their hatred. This realization makes Gordon experience a fear that is stronger than any he's ever felt. But even more than fear, in that moment he feels hatred, deep and immediate, for everyone in the room. And that hatred makes him feel alive. Gordon wants to live, and wants to walk out, and most of all he wants to see them all die. But to do that he has to get home. He wants to go home. He says, "I've got a family—"

Dujuan grabs him by the throat, and pushes the chair back on its two hind legs. "Say that shit again."

Gordon croaks, "—Don't do this to them—"

Dujuan spits, "—I know you got a family. I got a family, and look what you done to them. I oughta do the same to yours."

Dujuan releases the chair down on all fours.

Gordon thinks of Barbara and Janet and Tracey and Terry and Stewart, and flashes on images of what Dujuan would do to them. He says, "You are an evil young man."

"Maybe so," Dujuan replies. "But nothin compared to you."

✦

Malia calls Anthony. The phone rings and rings. No one answers.

She calls again the next day, and the day after, and the day after that.

No one answers.

✦

A moment later, Dujuan says to Gordon, "Tell you what. To show you what kind of a man I *really* am, I'm gonna to give you somethin my sister never had . . ."

Gordon looks at him carefully, then asks, "A second chance?"

"I'm gonna. . ." Dujuan trails off. He takes a deep breath, sniffs, then explodes, "Fuck! We gotta get out of here!"

Ray-Ray aims his gun at Malia, then barks, "Dujuan, is it her? She set us up?"

Quickly, "No. Not her."

Ray-Ray says, "Let's do this son of a bitch and get out of here."

"What's going on?" Malia asks.

Dujuan says, "Somebody comin. We gotta get him out of here."

Simon cuts Gordon loose. Gordon stands, held on either side by Ray-Ray and Simon. Malia looks around wildly, and her eyes fall on the Vexcorp file.

The outer door opens, then shuts. Simon quickly shuts the door to Malia's office. Ray-Ray says to Gordon, "Not a sound."

Malia calls out, "Dennis, is that you?"

Ray-Ray doesn't know who Dennis is. He doesn't like this.

There's a short silence before Ray-Ray hears a man's voice. "Yeah, it's me."

Malia says, "Don't come in."

Just outside the door, he asks, "What?"

Malia freezes for a moment, then says, "I'm . . . I'm not wearing any clothes."

Even Gordon stares at her.

Dennis opens the door, begins to enter, then stops in the doorway. He sways slightly. He's tall and slender. His face is red from drink. He says, "What?"

Ray-Ray points his gun at Dennis. Simon begins to laugh, then says to Malia, "You the worst fuckin liar I ever seen."

"What the hell was I supposed to say? 'Don't come in, we're holding Larry Gordon at gunpoint'?"

Dennis continues to sway, and stares at her. He's drunk near to the point of falling down. Ray-Ray doesn't like him.

Dennis asks, "You're holding Larry Gordon at gunpoint? What for? Are you going to shoot him?"

Malia says, "We were just getting to that."

"Are they gonna shoot you?"

"No."

"Are they gonna shoot me?"

"No." She looks at Dujuan, then says, "You're not going to shoot him."

Ray-Ray says, "Witness."

Dujuan smells the air, says, "Nah."

Ray-Ray answers, "We can't leave him."

"He won't talk. And he didn't do anything. I'm through hurtin people who don't deserve it."

Ray-Ray is dubious, but nods. He is, in a sense, relieved.

Dennis pulls out his cell phone.

Malia says quickly, "What are you doing?"

"Calling the cops."

Dujuan snatches the phone out of his hand.

"What did you do that for?" Dennis asks.

"You ain't gonna call the cops."

"I'm not. I'm not?"

"Your friend here will go to prison," Dujuan says.

"You haven't kidnapped her?"

"Look on the desk near her hand."

Dennis looks. "So?"

"Dujuan says patiently, "What do you see?"

"A gun."

"You seen many kidnap victims with guns?"

Dennis says, "Ok. No . . . Wait. I don't understand. What's happening?"

Malia says, "Larry Gordon's on trial."

"For?"

Dujuan says, "Killin my sister."

"He . . . ?"

Gordon says, "See? It's crazy."

Dujuan tells him to shut up.

Malia says, "His sister died of cancer. Vexcorp's effluents."

Dennis is sobering a little. He asks, "Are you out of your mind? You can't do this."

Dujuan responds, "Watch us."

Dennis says, "Malia, you can't . . . You never should have brought him here." He evidently isn't sobering much, because he sways and almost stumbles.

Ray-Ray wants to plug him just for being so drunk. He says to Malia, "You work with this guy?"

Malia shrugs.

Dennis says, "But Malia, I thought you believed in Democracy."

Dujuan responds, "That's what we're doing here."

Dennis stares hard at Dujuan, shakes him off, then says,

"Not here. Not like vigilantes. Not taking the law into your own hands."

Dujuan asks, "Whose hands should we leave it in? Yours?" He nods toward Gordon. "His? The cops?"

Dennis is silent.

Dujuan says, "Let's get back to what we were doin."

Dennis says, "Don't you understand? It's no good. None of this. You—all of you—think you can make some sort of difference by shooting this, this, this piece of . . . excrement. You're crazy. Another one will take his place, and then another, and another, and every one of them will poison away to his little heart's content, until there's nothing left on the planet but ashes and dust."

Malia says, "Gordon here was just trying to convince us to spare his life for that very same reason."

Dennis stares hard at Gordon before he says, "Huh, what do you know, me and Gordon think alike. I gotta tell you, though, it's a pretty stupid argument to make. If I'd have said something like that to my mom . . ."

Malia cuts him off gently, "We've already heard that one, Dennis."

Dennis thinks hard, then asks, "So what are you going to do about it?"

"Proceed."

"But Malia—"

Dujuan interjects, "He poisoned my sister."

Dennis responds, "Poison is wrong. Poison is definitely wrong. But you know what they say?" He pauses, then says, his voice severely slurred, "Go ahead, ask me. Has to do with two wrongs . . ."

Malia says, "I know what they say."

"Then don't do this. No violence. No violence. Nonviolence."

Malia spits, "Drop it, Dennis. Martin Luther King is dead. He got murdered."

Dujuan looks at Ray-Ray. Ray-Ray nods.

Dennis says, "Wait. You said this is a democracy. That's what you said. We gotta vote."

Dujuan looks at him like he's crazy.

Dennis continues, "Vote, count on our little fingers, you know? One guilty, two not guilty, three, and majority rules. It's a democracy, like the real thing."

Dujuan snorts. "Okay, I vote guilty."

Ray-Ray nods assent, and sees that Simon does, too. Ray-Ray doesn't understand why they're doing this. The fucker's guilty, responsible for Ricky's death—and for forcing Ray-Ray to pump him full of shit, and ultimately put him out of his misery—and for the death of Shameka, and for the deaths of so many others. Why didn't they just waste him in his car outside his home? That would have been so much cleaner, quicker. And they wouldn't have to listen to all this yammering. It seems words are only being used here to confuse the issue, which is that Gordon has killed more people than any of them can count, and so Gordon should die. Next time they kill a CEO they'll do it differently.

Ray-Ray catches himself, realizes how casually he'd been thinking of murder. Perhaps Dujuan's right: if Gordon's going to die, they should at least let him have his say first.

Dujuan turns to Gordon, who refuses to participate.

Dujuan says, "Fine. One whaddyacallit . . . abstention. The best you can hope for then is—"

Gordon cuts him off. "—I'll vote. Not guilty."

Dujuan looks at Dennis, who says, "Oh, he's guilty as hell, but guilty means you shoot him. So I vote not guilty."

Dujuan turns to Malia. "Three to two."

Malia asks him, "Are you really going to do this?"

"You mean, kill him?"

"No. Let him go if I vote no."

Dujuan doesn't say anything. If it comes to it, Ray-Ray knows Dujuan will have the balls to let him go. But he also knows it will never come to that.

Malia says, "If you let him go he'll tell the police."

"I can't help that."

"That's not an answer."

Dujuan responds, "It's my answer. I've had to disappear before."

"What about the others?"

"Ray-Ray and Simon? They'll be okay."

Ray-Ray thinks for a moment. He doesn't want to disappear, but if he has to he will.

"What about me?"

"You ain't gonna go to the cops."

"What if Dennis does?"

"That's yo problem."

Malia nods slowly. Then she asks, "What if instead of killing him or letting him go we hold him till Vexcorp reduces its pollution?"

Dujuan sneers, "Long as we being realistic, what do you think's gonna happen when we let him go?"

Malia's confused. "Cops?"

"No! Jesus. More pollution."

Through all of this Gordon is silent. Malia closes her eyes, then opens them again to look at Gordon.

He bursts out, "For God's sake, this is barbarism. You can't do this." Gordon continues, "Not you. Listen. You're—"

Malia says, "Guilty." Then she says it again.

No one moves. No one speaks.

Malia says, "But I can't kill him . . . Not for retribution. To stop him, I think so."

Dujuan looks at her. He says, "You think we let him go, he's gonna do anythin different?"

She has no answer.

Anthony finally picks up the telephone.
Malia says, "It's so good to hear your voice."
"Yours, too," he says.

Silence.

He asks, "Do you love me?"

"Of course."

"Do you still want to come visit me?"

"Of course."

"Do you love me enough that you would give up many things to see me?"

"Why are you asking me these questions?"

"I just want to know how much you want me."

"More than anything."

Silence.

"Are you sure?"

"Anthony, what is wrong with you?"

"I want you to come."

Larry Gordon remembers reading once that on the day of his execution, one of the English kings had requested an extra shirt so he wouldn't shiver from the cold. He hadn't wanted his enemies to be able to say he had trembled with fright. It seems important to Gordon to remember which king it was, but just right now he can't think of the name.

He thinks of Barbara, and wonders how she will take the news of his death. It will hit her hard, he thinks. And his children. Never again will he get to feel the hearth against his skin as he plays chess with Tracey, nor will he take the long walk to the park to shoot baskets with Janet. He will never get to see Terry go to school. And never again will he get to hunt with Stewart.

And he might never understand what it is that has nagged him all those sleepless nights. That bothers him, as though he's read part of a mystery that he knows he'll now never get to finish. But, he thinks, if I'm dead, I won't wonder anymore, will I?

He looks at Dujuan, "Will you at least let me say good-bye to my family?"

"You want us to let you make a phone call?"

"Just a note."

Dennis says, "Give him that much."

Dujuan nods. Malia stands, picks her gun off the desk, and slips it in her pocket. She says to Gordon, "Come around."

Gordon notices Ray-Ray and Simon watching him closely as he stands and circles the desk. He sits and picks up a pen. It's blue plastic, with white lettering advertising a local bank. The plastic is textured. He uses gold-tipped *Francesco Rubinato* pens at home. He wishes he could use one to write this letter. But, he supposes, at this point it doesn't really matter. He looks at Malia.

She says, "The paper's in the top right drawer."

He opens the drawer and pulls out a sheet. After looking at it for a moment, he says, with a weary smile, "I don't suppose you want me to use letterhead."

Malia responds softly, "The regular paper is in the back."

He reaches further, and pulls out a blank piece of paper. He puts it on the blotter. He looks at a photo on the desk. It's of a family. He asks, "Who's the little girl?"

Malia doesn't respond.

He says, "This must be Robin."

Malia still doesn't respond.

He says, "She's a beautiful child."

"How—"

"She lives with your parents, doesn't she? I really love that area. My family owns land up there. Did you know that?"

Malia doesn't say anything.

After a pause, Gordon says, "Sometimes I think we take you more seriously than you take yourselves."

Anthony can't sit. He can't stand. He is sick to his stomach. He has never done anything like this before.

He wishes the feds had never shown up, had never forced him to make this decision, forced him to do this.

✦

Dujuan doesn't mind giving Gordon the opportunity to write. There isn't a chance in hell he'll send the letter. This whole thing is already way too sloppy. Next time will be smoother. But right here and right now if Gordon is going to die, he may as well be given as much peace as possible.

Dujuan goes over in his mind what they'll do later. Clean the room, then dispose of the body by driving way the hell out of town, weighting it down, and dumping it in the river. The irony of this is too great—Gordon will be feeding the very fish he's poisoned—but far more important is that the body will probably never be found. Dujuan's sure that no one up at Gordon's had seen their car, but to be safe he'll get new tires—the old ones are bald anyway—so there'll be no match if the cops somehow get impressions of their tires on the asphalt at the beginning of Gordon's driveway. He doesn't think that's possible, but he's seen enough forensics cop shows to be worried about stuff like that. Because of those programs, he's decided also to scour the trunk to remove all traces of Gordon. He's not sure if this is overkill. With no body there will never be any reason for anyone to connect them with the killing. And he knows that if anyone does connect them to it, the cops certainly won't let a lack of real evidence stand in their way: he's already seen them plant too much. The key is to avoid the spotlight in the first place. Malia and Dennis are the real wild cards. But he's sure Malia won't turn them in. She's too heavily involved, and in any case he feels he knows her. At first he'd been frightened of what she'd awakened in him, and he'd thought he hated her for it, but even then he'd felt somehow connected to her. That only leaves Dennis, and Dujuan doesn't want to kill him for the simple crime of wandering into the office at the wrong time. That would make Dujuan no better than Gordon. This means he's going to have to trust his intuition, which is far different than trusting Dennis, something he would never have done.

Dujuan looks around the room. He, Malia, Simon, and

Ray-Ray form a rough square with Gordon at the center. Malia is on Dujuan's left, and Simon is on his right. Ray-Ray is opposite. Dennis stands between Ray-Ray and Simon. Gordon writes, then pauses, then writes. Dujuan looks over Gordon's shoulder.

Gordon asks, "Do you mind?"

"You know we're going to read it," Dujuan says.

Gordon thinks, nods, then continues to write. After a time he says, to Malia, "My son and I go deer hunting up in that area every fall. We've driven right by your parents' place." He pauses, then says, "He's an extraordinary young man. I am sorry I won't . ."

No one says anything for a moment. Dujuan breaks the silence: "You shoulda thought of that before you poisoned my sister."

Gordon heaves a deep sigh, then says, "This is all so wrong."

Another silence.

"There is so much I want to say to all of them," Gordon says. He turns to Malia and asks, "If you could never see your niece again, what would you say to her?"

After a moment, Malia says, "I think I would tell her I love her."

Gordon looks at the paper, briefly writes something, then puts down the pen.

Anthony feels better. Once committed to a course of action he rarely looks back. And besides, worrying isn't going to help anything.

Malia calls.

He says, "I'm so excited to see you!"

She says, "One more week!"

"I've been thinking about what I'd like for you to do when you get here."

"Do tell."

"Do you mind if I get graphic?"

"Please."

"*My fantasies lately have been running to licking honey off of your body.*"

"*Oh. My. Goddess.*"

"*Dripping it between your breasts, down your belly. But not so much that it gets all over the bed. Just enough to lick off.*"

"*You'd be amazed at how hot it's getting inside this phone booth.*"

"*Do you know one of my favorite memories of you? It's of you riding the honey extractor, your hair flowing back in the wind, your face so beautiful as you look at the honeycombs. I loved watching you, and the whole time I kept thinking I wanted to lick the honey off of you.*"

A heavy sigh on the other end of the phone. Then she says, "*You've said what you want to do when I get there, but not what you'd like me to do. Do you have any parts you'd like me to lick honey off of?*"

Anthony speaks slowly, as if relating a dream. "*Oh, I can think of so many places. I loved our lovemaking. Everytime was special between us.*"

"*Tell me one.*"

He begins to speak faster and faster as the dream or memory or whatever it is gains momentum. "*Do you remember the time we helped your father move bees to Charlie's house? Your father was migrating, and we helped him. And then a couple of days later the bees started stinging one of the neighbors and so we had to go over there right away. I was in town when you got the message but you were at your parents', so we had to meet over at Charlie's place. Do you remember that?*"

She just listens.

"*After we met there and got the bees all loaded we took them back, and do you remember how we made love that night? Do you remember the way we made love, the things we did, all the things we did?*

She says, quietly, "*Remind me.*"

"*Oh god, you took me in your mouth, and there was this thing you did, where you fluttered your tongue along the end.*"

"*I'm starting to remember.*"

"You did that all the time, but that night was special. I re-member later you were on your back and I was kissing your clitoris and you were about to come. But I didn't want you to come right there, and so you got on top of me. And I remember you sitting above me, me in-side of you, and you were leaning forward and you were moving slowly, and your hair hung down. I can remember the moonlight coming in through the window and I remember your face all in shadow. All these years I've held and cherished that image. What I would love for you to do is make more memories like that with me."

"I'd love that, too, Anthony."

Anthony stops, silent for a moment, then says, no longer lost in the image, "Isn't it strange how memory works? Somehow for all these years I've never been able to delink that image of making love with you from meeting up at Charlie's to move the bees."

"I know what you're talking about. It's kind of like what I wrote in those letters about not being able to delink any action from what came before." She laughs. "Maybe we even need to thank Charlie for us making love that way—"

Anthony interrupts her: "Exactly."

She continues, "Had we not driven out there we may not have made love exactly that way later on."

"I know. Isn't that strange? Or maybe there would have been some terrible accident or something."

"I think about that a lot," she says. "If it weren't for all sorts of small events, I never would have been associated with Larry Gordon's kidnapping. There are so many other examples."

"There are so many examples for all of us."

She pauses, then says, "I need to get off the phone."

"I miss you."

"I'll see you soon."

"Not soon enough."

Jessica shows Donald a transcript of the most recent phone call. He glosses over it, slows when he gets to the parts about Anthony kissing

Malia's clitoris, speeds up again till he gets to the end. Then he says, "This is perfect. We've got her. She admits on tape she was associated with the kidnapping."

"But we knew that already, didn't we, sir?"

"Now we have her admission on tape. She's finished. When we get her, she's getting the death penalty."

When we get her, *Jessica thinks.* When we get her.

The act of writing the letter to his family helps Gordon articulate the feeling that has nagged at him for so long. He feels the realization rising toward the surface, almost like a fish teasing its way toward a fly. Up and up, till you can make out the general shape, and then see the spots and red band running along its side. But it still won't come to the top.

He needs to say something. He knows that his realization will be wasted on the people in the room—*pearls before swine* is the phrase—but he knows also that the thought won't come to him unless he speaks it aloud. That's how he often works. The act of speaking forces the realization to declare itself. He says, quietly, "I get it."

Everyone looks at him.

Gordon starts to say, "I never understood until just now . ."

Dujuan asks, "What the fuck you talkin bout?"

Gordon replies, still speaking softly, "Money doesn't insulate you from loss."

Dujuan shakes his head, and spits, "It's about fuckin time."

Gordon had known they wouldn't understand. He almost wishes he hadn't said it. But he'd been saying it to himself. And he says, to himself also, "But I still don't want to die."

In the days before Malia's scheduled arrival, Jessica reads and rereads the transcript of that last conversation between Anthony and

Malia. Donald reads and rereads it, too, but she suspects for a different reason. Something bothers her about the conversation, but she can't quite figure out what it is. . . .

⊕

Donald Spaulding and Jessica Keller go to Anthony's home. Another car follows, this with a dog and handler inside. Donald and Jessica get out of their car. They walk to the door, knock. Anthony answers, glances at the other car, asks them in.

Donald asks, "Is everything set for tonight?"

Anthony responds, "Yes, it is."

"You know what you need to do?"

"I made the arrangements. That's all I thought I was supposed to do."

"Just stay out of the way when we come in. We don't want you to get shot."

"Shot?"

"We don't think there will be any need for that. But we always want to be safe."

Silence.

Donald continues, "So we'll need to ask you to take your dogs outside. With your permission we'll bring in a sniffer dog to make sure the house contains no guns."

"Guns?"

"Yes," Donald says. "It's not that we don't trust you. You've been very cooperative."

Anthony takes his dogs outside, sits, pets them. The handler brings in the sniffer dog, who finds nothing. The handler and dog leave. Anthony and the dogs come back inside.

Donald says, "We'll have agents posted in the woods, so if she runs she's in trouble. When she gets here, just keep her safe and calm until we come through the door."

⊕

Malia had thought—somehow hoped—that Gordon's realization would be that children are worth more than money. But she'd been disappointed. And that disappointment solidifies her faith that what she's doing—participating in murder—isn't the atrocity that so much of her believes it is.

She looks at Gordon, who's still lost in his realization. He continues silent, then suddenly jerks his head to face Dujuan. Malia sees Ray-Ray flinch at the movement, but Ray-Ray doesn't shoot.

Gordon says, now fully animated, "You said something about a second chance! Just before the drunk guy came in you were about to say something about a second chance."

Malia looks at Dujuan, whose face reveals no emotion. He doesn't move.

Gordon continues, but his energy begins to stall, "Before . . . You, you said . . . I don't . . . Really . . ."

"I said," Dujuan responds, "I would give you somethin my sister never had. But I want you to say it first."

Gordon shakes his head, uncomprehending.

"I want you to say, 'Somethin that you never . . .'"

"Something that I never . . ."

". . . gave . . ."

"Gave . . . your sister. You want to give me something that I never gave your sister."

"Very good," Dujuan says. "Now, I want to see what kinda man you really are. Remember when yo ass was in the trunk of my car? We had another car a few blocks away that followed us down. And what do you think was in the trunk of the other car?"

"I have no idea."

"How bout a little girl—" Dujuan says.

"—Who—"

"—the same age as my sister."

Malia says, "Dujuan?"

Dujuan gestures sharply to her, but she doesn't understand what the gesture's supposed to mean.

"Here's the deal," Dujuan says. "If you can do to her what

you did to my sister, you can walk."

"I can walk?"

Malia's throat tightens. Her breath comes in short catches. She hears her voice: "What are you doing?"

Dujuan gestures to her again, and then he says, "That's right. All you gotta do is shoot her once, in the head, and then you can go. You can tell the cops, you can tell the other board members, you can tell anybody you want about all this bullshit. You can go huntin with your kid every goddamn fall for the rest of your life. I don't care."

Malia says, "Dujuan, I won't allow this."

Dujuan turns to Malia and says, "This is my show, and I'm runnin it now. It was my sister. He thinks he's so tough. Let's see how damn tough he really is."

"I can walk," Gordon says again.

"You can crawl for all I care."

"Who is she?" Gordon asks.

"What's it to you? Has that ever mattered before?"

Malia begins to cry.

"We made it easy for you," Dujuan says. "We drugged her. You don't even have to look in her eyes."

"How stupid do you think I am?" Gordon asks. "You're going to frame me for this."

Dujuan smiles sardonically. "Would I do that?"

"My prints will be on the gun, and you'll just call the police."

"I'm gonna kidnap you, force you to kill a random kid, and then call the cops on you? You callin me stupid again?"

"You'll shoot me when I'm holding a gun."

Dujuan shakes his head in disgust. "You wanna walk or not?"

Malia is frozen. She can't act, can't even think. She looks to Dennis for help, but he stands mouth agape on the other side of the room. She wishes he would do something. She doesn't know what she can do alone.

"Maybe you want her to die," Gordon says.

"She means nothing to me."

Malia says, "Dujuan—"

Dujuan turns to her and says, "For the last time, Malia, stay out of this." He turns back to Gordon. "As of now you a dead man. You want to live or not?"

"I do it and I walk."

"Your choice."

After a long pause, Gordon says, "I want to live."

"Stand up," Dujuan says.

Everything begins to move very slowly. Malia sees every detail as Gordon leans slightly forward in the chair. She sees the way the folds in his jacket deepen and then disappear as he gains his feet. She sees the closed look in his eyes. Then Malia looks at Dujuan, and sees his face is blank. She sees Dujuan nod, barely perceptibly, to Ray-Ray. But she doesn't follow Dujuan's glance. Instead she acts instinctively, like the grizzly. She hears her voice make an inchoate scream as she pulls her pistol from her pocket and begins to fire at Gordon. She hears a loud pop as the first shot hits him in the left side of his chest and throws him off balance. Then another bullet strikes him, and then another, each pushing him further onto his heels. He staggers back a step, then leans forward, overcompensating. Malia's ears are ringing. She smells cordite. She turns, still in slow motion, to face Dujuan, who has stepped between her and Ray-Ray and is saying sharply to him, "I've got it. I'm in control. You follow my lead."

She sees Ray-Ray lower his gun.

Malia leans forward, still crying. She looks at Gordon, who continues to stand, and who looks at her blankly, with just a hint of surprise showing at the corners of his eyes. Three small red ovals stain his shirt. The shirt is torn in those spots, the ragged edge of fabric feeding into the dark red of the hole. Gordon's knees begin to buckle, and Simon slides a chair beneath him.

⊕

"This is the hardest part," Donald says to Jessica. "The waiting. The goddamn waiting."

She doesn't say anything.

It's very late, after five in the morning. Hours ago they'd seen the last of the lights go out in Anthony's home.

Jessica thinks she's figured it out.

Donald says, "Maybe she got lost. Maybe she forgot how to get here. Maybe she had car trouble somewhere."

"How much longer do you want to give her?"

"Let's give the bitch a few more hours."

Silence. Any desire to help Donald understand has disappeared.

"Nothing personal."

Gordon shakes his head slowly. He needs to make Malia understand that this isn't right. It's hard to breathe. He feels a powerful, dull ache in his chest, and a grainy feeling deep inside, as though someone were pulling his heart gently yet insistently into his abdomen, down into the deepest part of his body, pulling with hands of rough-hewn lumber, steel pipes, cotton, hands that had picked cotton, hands that had opened the circular valves at the refineries. Heavy. He feels a weight on his chest that compresses his ribs until each snaps in two. He hears Dujuan say, "It's okay. Shoot me if you want."

But Gordon doesn't want to shoot Dujuan. He wants to go home. He wants Barbara to hold him until he falls asleep.

Dujuan continues, "I'm sorry. I thought you knew."

There's no reason, Gordon thinks without words, to apologize. There's just been an accident, and someone has been shot. He doesn't know who. He's getting tired. His eyes flutter. He hears Malia say, "That you're a psychopath?"

Patterns of green and black and white. The all-seeing eye of God atop a pyramid. A tomb with God at the apex. That's it, he thinks. He understands now.

Dujuan says, "That there's no little girl."

Of course there's no little girl, Gordon thinks. His girls are older. There's a little boy. Terry. Five years old. He plays concentration. He picks out the cards. Gordon picks a seven of hearts and a four of diamonds. Terry's going to win. He reaches out with his chubby hands.

Gordon opens his eyes enough to see Malia slowly shaking her head. She doesn't understand. Gordon knows that.

Dujuan says, "My sister died afraid. He didn't. Remember? I kept my promise to him."

Dujuan's right. The buck didn't die afraid. It had watched him calmly as he walked up to shoot it in the head. It had known what was coming and accepted it. Gordon holds Stewart tight around the shoulders, and tells him everything is going to be fine.

Gordon hears another voice, the drunk man, speaking now slowly, carefully. He says, "Ray-Ray had a bead."

And then he hears Dujuan say, "You're no killer. Give me the gun. It's okay."

Of course it's okay. Larry Gordon isn't going to die. He feels sorry for the people who've been killed. He's glad that Malia had understood, and that she had shot Dujuan and then all the others, and that she had walked away and left him sitting in his chair. He's very comfortable. He's warm, and he no longer feels anyone pulling on his heart. He walks out of the office and gets in his car and this time he does not stop but instead drives home to Barbara and to his children. Barbara is watching a movie and he is in the movie and he is very tired and warm and he does not need to stay awake any longer.

Dujuan takes the gun from Malia's hand, then says to Ray-Ray and Simon, "Clean up time, boys. Bag him up and let's go."

Simon says, "The blood."

There isn't much of it. A little on the chair, spatters on the floor.

"I know," Dujuan answers. Then to Malia, "We'll take the chair with us. As for the rest, you got rags and cleaner?"

Dennis says, soberly, "In the closet off the main room."

Malia asks, "What are you going to do with him?"

Dujuan answers, "We're playin it by ear. But it's better you don't know."

Malia watches Ray-Ray and Simon pull garbage bags out of their pockets, and stuff Gordon's body into them. They have to tape the bags together.

After they carry the body from the room, Malia turns to Dennis and says, "I suppose you don't have any choice . . ."

Dennis wipes his hand across his forehead. Suddenly she sees the deep circles under his eyes. They must have been there all along. Or maybe now he's just losing color. He says, "About what? Turning you in? For what? I didn't see anything. I wasn't here. Nothing happened. I spent tonight getting wasted, and the next thing I knew I woke up with a hangover that would kill a rhino. I don't ever want to hear a word about this."

He turns to leave, then turns back to Dujuan. He says, "And I don't want to hear a word from you either. Never." He walks out the door.

Malia calls weakly after him, "Dennis! Do you want the Vexcorp file?"

Dennis sticks his head back in the door. For the first time she notices that his hair is standing up in front. He says, "I forgot to mention. I didn't come back for the file. I came to tell you that I got a nice long message from *60 Minutes*. Scheduling problems or some other shit, I forget."

"They're not . . ."

He continues, "Or maybe something about stock owner-ship and board interlocks. Who the fuck cares anymore?" He leaves Malia alone with Dujuan. She hears the outer door open and then close.

Malia asks, "What now?"

"I dunno. I thought I would," Dujuan says. "But I still

think I did a good thing."

When Malia finally answers, she says, "We did."

After that she takes a few steps around the room, which becomes blurrier moment by moment. The walls seem to spin, and she staggers, then leans heavily against her desk. The palms of her hands feel hot, and she begins to rub them hard against the front of her pants along her thighs. In some vague, distant, part of her mind she sees Dujuan standing unmoving, and she knows he wants to comfort her but doesn't know how. She sees Ray-Ray step into the doorway, holding cleaning materials. Malia begins to tremble, and her shoulders begin to move up and down. She bites hard at her lip to keep from breaking down. Putting her hands together she rubs hard, one palm against the other, and keeps rubbing.

Malia stands at the bus stop where she'd been mugged the previous spring. It's late. She's been working. She's on her way home. The night is hot. The street is empty. She hears the soft sound of sneakers on concrete, and turns to see a man walking toward her. For a moment, she wishes her pistol were in her hand and not in her backpack, but then she sees who it is. She says, "Hello, Simon."

Simon pauses before he says, "I didn't recognize you."

"You're still here," she says.

"I live here."

She asks, "Where are Dujuan and Ray-Ray?"

Simon says, "They don't do this bullshit no more."

Malia asks, "What bullshit?" Then she realizes what he's talking about. She says, "You weren't going to . . ."

Simon laughs. "Would I do that?"

She scowls and wishes again she had the gun. She doesn't trust Simon.

He says, "Dujuan and Ray-Ray aren't around so much these days. They doin some different shit. Gettin real political, you know what I'm sayin? Cloak and dagger type stuff. Wit different people. I don't hardly see them. And you remember that list? That was real. He's workin on that."

"Why didn't you go with him?"

Simon looks at her uncomfortably, and she knows from his look the answer to her question. There's silence for a moment, before Simon suddenly asks, "What about you?"

"Do I see Dujuan and Ray-Ray?"

"No, what are you doin?"

She says, "Next week I quit my job."

"You ain't gonna stop cancer?"

"Not this way."

Malia looks more closely at Simon. His skin is breaking out, and he looks pale.

part six

He says, "So, what . . ."

"My mom is dying. I'm going to be with my parents. I'll spend some time, figure out what's next."

Simon asks, "The cops ever, you know? . . ."

She shakes her head. "None. You?"

"No more than usual."

A car drives by. Neither speaks. Finally, Simon says, "I guess I should go." He begins to walk away. He gets only a few steps when he turns back to Malia and says, "I gotta know. Did it make a difference?"

Malia looks at him hard, then looks away. Then she brings her eyes back to his, and says, "The company's not going to fold or anything, but they put off their expansion . . . Indefinitely."

Simon smiles and says, "No shit. Because of us?" He begins again to walk away.

Malia calls after him, "Wait! If you see Dujuan, tell him I want to talk to him."

Simon smiles slyly, and says, "'Bout?"

"Tell him I want to help."

"How will he find you?"

"He'll figure it out."

As he walks away, Malia thinks, *It's really starting. It's really starting.*

It is morning. Jessica is dozing. She feels someone poke her arm. She hears a voice say, "Jessica."

She jerks awake, says, "Is she here?"

"No."

"Did she call?"

"The phone tappers say no."

Jessica is neither surprised nor disappointed. She thinks she knows exactly where Malia is. And she thinks she knows what will happen next. She says, "How much longer do we give this?"

"A couple more hours, tops. Then we call it off. She got

spooked. Or we got had. Or something. Maybe we got lucky and she died in a fucking car wreck. I just know we can't cover much more overtime on this dead end."

That's the answer she expected. She asks, "How much longer will we keep him under surveillance?"

"Phone taps? Forever. How much longer do we keep someone at his house? Tomorrow. We can't follow him around to the fucking grocery store, the hardware store, the post office. Not unless you want to do it on your own time. You got a hunch or something?"

"Like you said, sir, he's a dead end."

"That's what I said."

Two hours later they drive their rented car to the house. They get out. They walk to the door. They knock. No answer. They knock again. Still no answer. Donald says, "He couldn't have run. . . ."

The door opens. Anthony is there. He looks confused, finally says, "I thought you might be. . . ."

"Your girlfriend? Sorry. Looks like she didn't love you quite as much as she said."

"I don't know. . . ."

Donald thinks a moment, says, "No, I don't think you do. I wonder what other lies she told you all along. . . ."

"I would have no way of knowing."

Jessica wants to laugh out loud at Donald, for his pathetic attempt at using cruelty to mask his own failure. She wants to let Anthony know she knows, but at this point also knows that the use of any key words would unnecessarily frighten him, and might set Donald to thinking. And the last thing she wants is to start Donald thinking. But she can't help herself. And she figures she can assist Anthony in one way. She says, "The operation here is over. We're leaving the next couple of days, and after that, I trust you'll let us know if your honey contacts you."

Both Anthony and Donald give her strange looks. Anthony hides his quickly. Looking at her, Donald doesn't see it.

She says, "Or honestly, you're probably smart enough to figure we'll maintain phone coverage, so if she calls, we'll know before you do."

Donald says, "What are you. . . .?"

"He's not stupid."

Donald doesn't say another word. She knows she'll hear about it in the car, and on the plane, and she knows he'll write her up for this: Donald has to tie someone to the whipping post over this one.

And this time she doesn't mind at all if it's her.

It is four days later. Anthony drives into town. As he did once before, he drives in large multi-block loops, he drives in straight lines, he suddenly turns left or suddenly turns right. When at last he is convinced that no one is following him, he parks this time about a mile from the home of his friend Charlie. He walks the rest of the way.

Malia is waiting for him.

Charlie tells him that she will go out tomorrow and pick up the dogs and cats, and will take good care of them till they die.

Malia and Anthony get in Malia's car, and they begin to drive.

They drive a thousand miles, and tell each other about what they've done in the years in between. They stop at a rest area. Anthony asks Malia if she brought any honey.

She smiles, says, "There's plenty of honey at the safehouse."

He nods, they drive. He asks, "Are you still in contact with Dujuan and Ray-Ray?"

"I can be."

"You mentioned Dujuan's list. Does he still have it?"

"The original list is shorter now."

"He's got other lists?"

"We all do. And they're not just people. They're corporations, factories, pieces of infrastructure."

"How can I help?"

She smiles.

Special thanks to the Wallace Global Fund
for their ongoing support.

About Flashpoint Press

Flashpoint Press was founded by Derrick Jensen to ignite a resistance movement. Our planet is under serious threat from industrial civilization, with its consumption of biotic communities, production of greenhouse gases and environmental toxins, and destruction of human rights and human-scale cultures around the globe. This system will not stop voluntarily, and it can not be reformed.

Flashpoint Press believes that the Left has severely limited its strategic thinking, by insisting on education, lifestyle change and techno-fixes as the only viable and ethical options. None of these responses can address the scale of the emergency now facing our planet. We need both a serious resistance movement and a supporting culture of resistance that can inspire and protect frontline activists. Flashpoint embraces the necessity of all levels of action, from cultural work to militant confrontation. We also intend to win.

FLASHPOINT PRESS
CRESCENT CITY, CALIFORNIA

About PM

PM Press was founded at the end of 2007 by a small collection of folks with decades of publishing, media, and organizing experience. PM co-founder Ramsey Kanaan started AK Press as a young teenager in Scotland almost 30 years ago and, together with his fellow PM Press co-conspirators, has published and distributed hundreds of books, pamphlets, CDs, and DVDs. Members of PM have founded enduring book fairs, spearheaded victorious tenant organizing campaigns, and worked closely with bookstores, academic conferences, and even rock bands to deliver political and challenging ideas to all walks of life. We're old enough to know what we're doing and young enough to know what's at stake.

We seek to create radical and stimulating fiction and non-fiction books, pamphlets, t-shirts, visual and audio materials to entertain, educate and inspire you. We aim to distribute these through every available channel with every available technology - whether that means you are seeing anarchist classics at our bookfair stalls; reading our latest vegan cookbook at the café; downloading geeky fiction e-books; or digging new music and timely videos from our website.

PM Press is always on the lookout for talented and skilled volunteers, artists, activists and writers to work with. If you have a great idea for a project or can contribute in some way, please get in touch.

PM Press
PO Box 23912
Oakland, CA 94623
www.pmpress.org

Friends of PM

These are indisputably momentous times – the financial system is melting down globally and the Empire is stumbling. Now more than ever there is a vital need for radical ideas.

In the year since its founding – and on a mere shoestring – PM Press has risen to the formidable challenge of publishing and distributing knowledge and entertainment for the struggles ahead. With over 75 releases to date, we have published an impressive and stimulating array of literature, art, music, politics, and culture. Using every available medium, we've succeeded in connecting those hungry for ideas and information to those putting them into practice.

Friends of PM allows you to directly help impact, amplify, and revitalize the discourse and actions of radical writers, filmmakers, and artists. It provides us with a stable foundation from which we can build upon our early successes and provides a much-needed subsidy for the materials that can't necessarily pay their own way. You can help make that happen--and receive every new title automatically delivered to your door once a month--by joining as a Friend of PM Press. Here are your options:

$25 a month: Get all books and pamphlets plus 50% discount on all webstore purchases

$25 a month: Get all CDs and DVDs plus 50% discount on all webstore purchases

$40 a month: Get all PM Press releases plus 50% discount on all webstore purchases

$100 a month: Sustainer - Everything plus PM merchandise, free downloads, and 50% discount on all webstore purchases

Your Visa or Mastercard will be billed once a month, until you tell us to stop. Or until our efforts succeed in bringing the revolution around. Or the financial meltdown of Capital makes plastic redundant. Whichever comes first.

For more information on the *Friends of PM*, and about sponsoring particular projects, please go to www.pmpress.org, or contact us at info@pmpress.org.